DEREK'S CHRISTMAS CAROL

A Swept Away, Special Edition

ROSEMARY WILLHIDE

WWW.LUMINOSITYPUBLISHING.COM

LUMINOSITY PUBLISHING LLP

DEREK'S CHRISTMAS CAROL
A Swept Away, Special Edition
Copyright © December 2015 Rosemary Willhide
Paperback ISBN: 978-1-910899-51-9

Cover Art by Poppy Designs

Dedication

Derek's Christmas Carol is dedicated to all my readers who said, "Can we have more Derek and Nia?" I was so touched by your support for my debut series, I simply could not say no. For all the amazing women on my street team, in my reader group, and my friends in Hot BBR, thank you, for your hard work and your friendship. And to all of you who took a chance on a new author and were *Swept Away* into Nia and Derek's world, you have my eternal gratitude. When you write a book, you give away a little piece of your heart and soul. Thank you so much for embracing it, coming along on this journey, and being a part of my world. This one's for you.

Chapter One

Brooke and Tom's wedding reception was well underway as I glided Nia across the dance floor. It was December 1, nearly a year since Nia became my wife—my sexy as fuck, mischievous little wife. With our bodies sealed together, she deliberately, gyrated her hips gainst me, until she gave me a full-blown erection, just because she could. She had me and my dick wrapped around her finger, and I fucking loved it.

I whispered into her ear, "You're being a very a naughty girl."

She peeked up at me with that adorable grin. "I thought you liked my bad girl ways, husband."

"You know I do, angel. I would just prefer we were home, alone."

"And I was totally nakey?"

"Yes. Nakey. That's cute. I like it." I pressed my lips to her forehead, and my gorgeous, control freak attempted to lead while we swayed to our song "Unforgettable;" just like she did during our first dance at the charity event. I gripped her hips. "Young lady, who's in charge here? Do we need a reminder?"

"I might need a little discipline. After all, you bought that flogger for Naked Thanksgiving and we didn't use it."

"That's because you bought a paddle. If you recall, after my hand, the crop, and the paddle, your bottom was beet red."

Her cheeks blushed a deep shade of pink. "It was spankalicious. And so romantic. Me giving you the paddle, and you with the flogger. It was just like *The*

Gift of the Magi, only on Thanksgiving, with turkey, and kinky fucking."

I laughed and took the lead while our song changed keys, heading to the last verse. "Well, here's something to keep in mind, good girls get flogged too."

Nia's beautiful dark eyes grew wide with curiosity. "They do?"

"Of course. And when they are really good, they get to come."

She furrowed her brow. "You're not going to let me come tonight?"

"That, my sweet girl, is totally up to you. Do you think you can behave yourself the rest of the evening?"

She fluttered her eyes lashes at me. "Define 'behave,' Mr. Pierce."

I shook my head, and held her even tighter. "Do you have any idea how much I love you? I can't wait until our anniversary on Christmas Eve. I'm going to spoil you rotten. No arguments."

"Not a one. Not after everything we went through before the wedding. The breakup, and Larry Wall ... and... I..."

"Shhh ... baby." She buried her head in my chest with a sigh. "Hey, why are you bringing this up? What's going on?"

"Nothing," she mumbled.

"I need you to talk to me, angel. Nia. Look at me."

Tears welled up in her eyes. "I'm just being silly, but when you mentioned Christmas Eve, it reminded me you're leaving soon to film the finale of your new show on location in Japan. We've been together almost every day since we got married. I just don't want to think about being apart for ten days, especially so close to our first wedding anniversary. Japan is so far away. What if something happens, and you can't get back to Vegas in time?"

"Baby, nothing's going to happen. I promise. Would you feel better if you came with me?"

"I can't. Since you and Jake are going to be out of town, Lacey and I are teaching all the fitness classes. We wanted to keep ourselves busy while you guys were in Japan. I don't think the new owner of The Mountain Heights Country Club would like it if I shirked my responsibilities."

"You mean The Vegas Edge Country Club. Remember, Adam Maxwell changed the name."

"Well, it will always be Mountain Heights to me. The place where we met. I'll never forget the day devastatingly handsome Hollywood heartthrob, Derek Pierce, came to take my spin class."

I stroked her long, chocolate brown hair. "It was the best day of my life, and the best ass kicking in a spin class I ever got. I remember thinking, 'this tiny girl is wiping the floor with me.' I could barely keep up."

"I was so nervous. I was sure you thought I was a babbling idiot."

"Quite the opposite. I was charmed from the minute you opened your mouth."

She flashed me a smile so full of mischief it made my cock twitch. "Even when I said, 'Son of a bitch?'"

"Especially, when you said, 'Son of a bitch.' Hmm ... that dirty little mouth of yours."

I brought my lips down on hers, and with just one kiss, my dick strained against my trousers, begging to fuck her. God, what this woman did to me. Since the first time I was buried deep inside her tight, hot pussy, I knew I could never get enough of my Nia. As our kiss intensified, I grasped the nape of her neck, holding her to me, almost forgetting we were in public. She released a soft moan. Her panties were probably soaked by now. I broke our kiss, and my girl possessed that wild look in her eyes I loved. The one that said, she was mine for the taking. Nia and her pussy belonged to me.

"Christ, baby. What is it about you in this green dress? I'm ready to fuck you right here."

She caught her breath. "You can. I haven't seen Brooke since they cut the cake, so my bridesmaid's duties are finished. I'm sure no one would miss us if we snuck into the private dining room."

I nuzzled her neck. "Hmm ... are you wet for me?"

"Yes," she gasped.

"Then, go to the bathroom, take off your panties, and wait for me in the private dining room. I want you to pull up your dress to your waist, sit on the table, and spread yourself for me. I'm still hungry. I need something to eat."

Her skin pebbled and she swallowed hard. "Okay."

"I just have to touch base with Jake. I won't be long." I patted her bottom and sent her on her way.

I spotted Jake and Lacey at the bar grabbing another drink, and joined them. Jake hid his glass of champagne behind his arm. "Hey, boss. Where's Nia?"

"She ... uh ... went to the ladies room. Jake, you're off duty. There's no need to hide your drink from me. Brooke and Tom have arranged limos for all of their guests."

Lacey elbowed him. "See, I told you. It's no big deal. I bet you didn't think Jake was a champagne drinker."

"Not exactly," I said.

"It was always whiskey or beer for me. Then, Nia suggested I buy some *Veuve Clicquot* the night I proposed to Lacey." Jake snaked his arm around her waist. "Now every time I drink it, it reminds me of that night."

"That's so sweet," Lacey exclaimed.

"I'm glad you think so, babe." He tossed back his champagne as if it was water. "I was nervous as fuck."

I signaled for Al, the bartender. "I'll have what they're having. We should toast to you two, and to being 'nervous as fuck' when you propose. We've all been there, my friend. By the way, did you set the date yet?"

"Not yet," Lacey responded as we clinked glasses. "We're going to wait until he gets back from Japan."

"That's what I wanted to talk you about, Jake. I'd like you to assume more responsibility when we're there. I'm putting you in charge of security on set. Is that okay with you?"

Jake nodded. "Hell, yeah. That's more than okay. Thank you."

Lacey craned her neck toward the door. "Oh my God! Look at Keith and Tim. They're busting a gut about something and taking off. I wonder what happened."

"I'm sure there's a story there," I said. "Speaking of taking off, I better see what is keeping Nia. I'll be right back."

Before I could head to the private dining room to eat my wife's pussy, she was already marching toward us with a head full of steam. She maneuvered through the crowd like a pissed-off Miss Pacman.

In what seemed like two seconds she was at the bar fuming. She gritted her teeth. "Where *were* you?"

I lowered my voice. "I was just on my way to find you. What's got you all wound up?"

She shoved her wet panties in my hand. "Oh, nothing. I was just following orders when Keith and Tim flew through the door of the private dining room and saw me spread out on the table like I was part of the dessert buffet."

Jake and Lacey pretended not to hear and turned their attention to their champagne. I grasped her elbow and pulled her toward me. "Did they see you?"

She blurted out, "What do you think? They flipped on the light, and there was me and my 'Leave it to Beaver' out for the world to see."

I bit the side of my mouth to keep from laughing. Lacey's shoulders shook and Jake laid his head on the bar.

Nia couldn't contain her exasperation. "You guys. This is so the opposite of funny. Derek, are you laughing?"

I coughed and hid my face. "No. Of course not. I'm sure Keith and Tim were just as embarrassed as you."

"More like horrified. Keith turned white, and Tim said, 'Nia, we can see your *Hello Kitty.*' Then they cracked up and fled the scene like they were escaping prison."

By this point even the bartender, Al, was red faced, and wiping his eyes. Nia gave into the hilarity of the moment. "I guess it is a little funny. Although, I probably scarred them for life. Those two will never eat at the Pink Taco again."

We all enjoyed a hearty laugh, and Al poured Nia some champagne. "Thank you," she said. "I love *Veuve Clicquot.* If you wouldn't mind leaving the bottle, Al, I'm sure I'll need a refill in a hot minute."

"Not a problem," he replied. "In fact, Brooke instructed us to give the leftover cases to the bridal party. It's your gift for being part of the wedding. Just let us know when you're leaving, I'll make sure Matty, the bar back, takes care of it for you."

"That's way too generous," Lacey responded. "But who are we to turn down free *Veuve.* I want to thank her."

Julia and Phillip joined us at the bar, along with their sleeping baby boy.

"Good luck. I haven't seen them since they cut the cake," Nia said, and swigged her champagne. "Julia, have you seen them?"

"They left," Julia answered. "They snuck out and are probably at the airport by now. It was all part of Brooke's plan."

"But we didn't get to say good-bye," Nia replied.

"Yup. That was her plan. She was afraid she'd get too emotional with her family here and everything. She said she wanted to make the most of every moment and then slip out."

I raised a glass. "Well, here's to Brooke and Tom. It was a great party. Julia, if I didn't get a chance to tell you today, you look beautiful."

She smiled. "More like exhausted. This little cherub kept me up last night."

Phillip draped his arm around Julia's shoulder. "But you must admit, my little man was a real trouper today. Best ring-bearer in the history of weddings."

Joshua Phillip Dickson was almost three months old. He was a happy, healthy baby with a decent set of lungs. Watching Nia with him these past few months mesmerized me. She was such a natural but said several times she wasn't sure if she was ready to be a mother.

"He sure was." Nia hopped off her barstool to get a closer look at Joshua in his carrier. "Joshy, you were precious. Wow! He's out like a light. Bless his heart."

Julia looked on with sweet admiration. "He sure is. And we want him to stay that way so I can get some sleep."

Phillip interjected, "We're going to head home. We just wanted to say goodnight."

Nia linked arms with Julia. "Let me walk you guys out. Derek, I'll be right back. Tell Al to fill my champagne glass."

"Nice try," I said. "Someone has already had plenty to drink tonight."

I didn't like it when my girl drank too much. I wanted all her senses on high alert, especially for what I planned when we got home. Plus, she was so tiny. She'd go from tipsy to drunk in a few sips.

I said goodnight to Lacey and Jake and awaited Nia's return. The crowd really dwindled. The Petersons were out on the dance floor, with only a few other couples.

"Hi. You're Derek Pierce?" said a guy, about my age, close to my height, with dark hair.

"Yes. I know you, don't, I? Sorry, I'm drawing a blank on your name."

He offered his hand. "I'm Adam. Adam Maxwell."

"Of course." We exchanged a firm handshake. "Good to finally meet you. I love what you've done with the club. Home prices have doubled since you took over and changed the name to The Vegas Edge."

"Thank you. It's what I enjoy doing. Taking properties to extraordinary levels of greatness. I've had a good deal of success on the Strip. So far I heard the members and employees at the country club are pleased."

"Very." I motioned for Al to pour Adam some champagne. "I'm assuming you've met my wife, Nia? She works for you. She's the fitness coordinator."

"Actually, aside from Brooke and Tom, I know very few employees. My focus is back on the Strip. I have my eye on a new property that could use a facelift." He sipped his champagne, leaned toward me, and lowered his voice. "But, I noticed you dancing with your wife. She's lovely. What an exquisite submissive you have."

"A submissive?" I regarded him cautiously. "I'm not exactly sure what you're getting at."

"My apologies if I'm wrong. But, Sue Peterson mentioned you two might be interested in going to The Purple Peacock. It's a BDSM club. So ... naturally I assumed. Plus, there's a certain connection and energy I observed between you two. I'm not usually wrong about spotting someone in the lifestyle."

I relaxed my stance and took a seat. "Oh, yes, Nia has expressed her curiosity with The Purple Peacock. My girl is obedient to a point, inside the bedroom, but outside... She's a pill."

Adam chuckled knowingly. "For me, there's nothing like a feisty submissive. It's all the sweeter when they surrender control."

"Nia has the market cornered on feisty. I wouldn't necessarily call her a submissive, but I wouldn't have her any other way. The truth is, I'm the one dragging my feet about going to The Purple Peacock. When you're in the public eye, you can't be too careful. I'm sure you understand, being a prominent figure in Vegas yourself. There is such a thing as bad press."

"I agree. That's why the club is by invite only. I'm a silent partner, and I assure you, privacy is one of our main priorities. Any night you'd like to come, just let me know. I will screen each patron myself if you like."

"Well, Nia says going to a BDSM club is on her sex bucket list. God knows I can't say no to her."

He paused momentarily and sat his glass on the bar. "Then, I'd like to ask you something else, if I may?"

"Go for it."

He pulled up a bar stool and looked me right in the eye. "Has she ever expressed any interest in being shared? With your permission, we could give her a night she'd never forget."

I leaped to my feet, towering over him. "No one touches my wife. She's mine. She belongs to me."

"Understood. Nia is yours. I apologize if I overstepped. I would have kicked myself if I didn't at least ask. It can be considered a common question for those in my lifestyle or couples that are curious."

I backed off. "I didn't realize. So, what are we in for at The Purple Peacock, a mega orgy?"

"Did you say mega orgy?" Nia sidled up next to me. When she took in a complete view of Adam Maxwell her mouth gaped open, and her eyes bugged out of her head. I'd only seen her make this exact expression once—the night she met me. I didn't care for her open lustful gaze on my new acquaintance. Was he that good looking?

I pressed my hand into the small of her back. "Nia, this is your boss, Adam Maxwell."

She offered her hand, and her voice turned squeaky. "Hi, Nia. I mean, Mr. Maxwell. It's nice to meet you. I'm Nia Kelly ... Pierce. I'm Nia Pierce. I almost forgot. I'm married." She let out a nervous laugh.

Obviously charmed by her, he placed his hand on top of hers. "It's nice to meet you, Married Nia Pierce. Please, call me Adam. Your husband and I were just discussing that you two might be interested in a visit to The Purple Peacock. It's the BDSM club that Sue Peterson mentioned to you. I'm a silent partner, and I'd love to have you ... at the club."

Finally, they disengaged their handshake, and Nia peeked up at me. "Really? What did the old ball and chain say?"

I coiled my arm around her waist and whispered in her ear, "Careful, young lady. I have a flogger."

"It seems we've reached an understanding," Adam said. "Just let me know what night you'd like to come.

I'll arrange something special for you. You have my word, everything will be handled with absolute discretion."

Nia's hand found its way into my coat pocket, where I'd previously squirreled away her sodden panties. She fingered them and brushed those damp digits over her lips, suggestively. "So, it's like BDSM on the down low. What do I wear, leather chaps and a bra with spikes?"

Adam smiled. "Not unless you want to advertise to everyone that it's your first time. As I recall, the Petersons made that mistake. Just wear whatever you would wear to any other club. The dress you have on is beautiful on you."

Nia giggled. "Thank you."

Not wanting the flagrant flirting to go on a second longer, I put an end to it. "We'll be in touch about the club. Thank you for the offer."

Receiving my message loud and clear, Adam gave us his card and said goodnight.

Nia waved Al over. "If we're going to that club, we should drink to it. More bubbles, please."

Al filled her glass. "Anything for you, Mrs. Pierce. Oh, and Matty loaded a couple cases of *Veuve Clicquot* in your limo. We figured you two would be heading out soon. We didn't want you to have to wait."

Nia picked up her glass. "Thank you. As soon as I toss this back we'll get out of your hair."

"Take your time," Al responded, and left us on our own.

"Just what do you think you're doing?" I asked.

She took a big gulp from her glass. "Drinking this delicious beverage, that was already poured. It would be a shame to waste it."

"What did I tell you earlier?"

She shrugged. "That you had a flogger. And, you were going to let me come."

"Nice try. I believe I said whether or not you came depended on you. Do you think you behaved by drinking more champagne, after I asked you not to?"

"Well, I can't un-drink it."

"Then I suggest you do not take another sip."

She held the glass to her lips with a defiant, sexy glare. "Things just got interesting."

* * * *

"Well, well, well. Did someone deliberately disobey me?" I asked.

Nia was trussed to the bed, wearing nothing but a blindfold, completely at my mercy. Her legs spread wide, giving me access to her already glistening pussy. Tonight, I would tease her to new limits for the little stunt at the bar. She needed to be taught a lesson. Between the flogger, the restraints, and one other surprise I had in store, she would be strung out in unrelenting need, begging me to let her come.

She tugged on her secure ties. "Am I going to be punished?"

"Yes, angel. You are."

"If this is the 'no coming' punishment, I'd like to negotiate."

I couldn't help but be amused by her. She had zero control over the situation, and she still couldn't keep her mouth shut.

I whispered in her ear, "No negotiating, sweet girl. Tell me, who owns that pussy?"

She licked her lips. "You do. It's yours."

I ran my fingertip along her jawline. "Good girl. You may get to come after all."

Her chest heaved and her irresistible nipples protruded like two ripe buds. I took them in my mouth, but just long enough to make her whimper, then I stopped, leaving her wanting. Her body squirmed and yet settled into the mattress. She was ready for what I planned.

I picked up the black and white flogger, grazing it lightly over her stomach. "Feel that, baby?"

Her hips careened and swayed with the movement of the flogger, leaving a trail of goose bumps. "Mmm ... it feels good."

The black leather would sting, but the white fur would be more gentle. It was just like her, naughty and nice. I continued exploring every inch of her skin while she basked in the anticipation of the first strike. The way her breathing changed and her skin flushed, told me it was all systems go.

I brought the flogger down on her stomach with medium force, and Nia yelped in surprise. I lashed her inner thighs, watching her revel in that sweet spot— where pain met pleasure.

I ceased and checked her pussy, by spreading her outer lips and skimming my fingers along her slit. "Just as I thought. You're drenched. You look delicious. I need a taste." I circled my tongue over her plump clit. "Hmm ... so saucy ... so good. It's selfish of me not share." I pushed two fingers into her dripping cunt, and she cried out. If I wanted to, I could've had her coming in two seconds, but not tonight.

I brought my fingers to her mouth. "Here, baby. Suck."

She gasped, "Oh ... yeah."

She opened up for me and guzzled the juiced digits inside. *Christ.* The sight of her sampling her own essence while bound and blindfolded was one of the most fucking erotic things I'd ever seen. I allowed her to ride my other hand with her pussy, just long enough to ramp her up even further.

I retracted my fingers. "Good girl. Does my angel like the way she tastes?"

"Yes. Can I have more?"

I brushed her cheek with the back of my hand. "We'll see." I grabbed the flogger and slapped it over stomach four times, each a little harder than the last. Then I distributed swats evenly over both legs. Nia's reaction made my dick twitch and throb. I palmed my steely girth, and my balls clenched, thinking about the damage I would do with my cock when I thoroughly fucked one of her holes.

I lightly tapped the leathery fur strands on her pussy, and her body jerked against the restraints. Jesus, she was so sexy, reeling in her beautiful agony.

Again my tongue lapped up her juices. It was like drinking from a fountain of liquid honey.

"Derek, please. I'm begging you. Please let me come. Ah ... yeah... Ah ... yeah... I'm so close."

That was my cue to stop. But I couldn't resist taking possession of her mouth, and pouring all my aching lust into one long kiss that left her breathless.

Her breasts were my next target. My hands fondled them, making her nipples as hard as two silver bullets. I rolled each one between my fingers, pinching, turning, and pulling. Then, quickly released her pretty firm flesh, keeping her edged out and in crazy arousal.

It was like a game of bait and switch. Her responsive body was an orgasmic, squirting, Arcadia. During our honeymoon in London, she had to go to the bathroom while dining at a restaurant inside the Shard and remove her wet panties. Maybe it was the incredible panoramic views, but she came during a deep kiss, at the Oblix. It was one of the few times we left our suite at The Ritz, besides going to Westminster.

Nia made me laugh when she joked she was disappointed that Big Ben was just a clock. When I wrapped her up in my arms, she felt my hardening erection pressing into her, and it was back to the hotel for round three or seven. An invite from the Queen wouldn't have stopped us. It was an all-out ten-day fuck-a-thon.

Now, I had her right where I wanted her—racked with needy desire. It was the perfect moment to introduce Nia to a new toy, one that would render her old friend, Buzz the vibrator, useless. Not that she was permitted to come without me, but he was occasionally invited to join the fun when I took her sweet, little ass.

The room grew quiet as I scuffed across the carpet, opened one of our many kink drawers, and pulled out the magic wand. According to Jake, the effect of this pulsating, bulbous-shaped head had on Lacey was unmatched by anything else. It must be ten times more powerful than Buzz. After all, it plugged into the wall. Knowing my greedy girl, this should remain under lock and key.

"Derek." She heaved. "What are you doing? You can't possibly leave me like this."

I plugged in the wand and placed it on the bed. "Leave you like what, angel?"

"So ... oh God... I need to come, so bad. Please. Do you want me to beg? I'll beg."

I checked the snugness of the blindfold, and traced my fingertips over her luscious, full lips. "I wanted you to behave. What did you do?"

"I was naughty. I went too far drinking the glass of champagne. I should be disciplined."

I brushed my hand over her exquisite collarbones and marveled at her toned beauty. "You will be disciplined, and teased to new limits tonight. Just give into me, Nia. You know I always take care of my baby.

But you're going to need to be patient. Do you understand?"

"I understand." A serene expression fell across her face. A look I'd seen before, during our playtime. She was in that headspace where her body could let go. I fired up the wand.

Nia flinched. "Holy fuck! What's that noise? Are you going to suction my pussy with a leaf blower?"

I held back a chuckle. She had a point. This thing was loud—even on the lowest setting. Hopefully, our dog, Molly, was still busy destroying a new toy, or the sound of the new vibrator would have her scratching at the door in no time.

"Relax," I told her, and my girl obeyed. Her limbs fell more slack, and she licked her lips and sighed.

Armed with the wand in one hand, I rubbed her swollen, sensitive, flesh, with the other, getting her ready for the impending sensation. Prying her pussy lips open wide, I lightly touched the wand to the tip of her clit, and she shrieked in agonizing passionate cries. I'd never heard her be so animalistic before.

"Jesus, fuck. Ah ... fuck, fuck, fuck!"

I turned the toy off and kept her on the edge of orgasm with tender strokes of my hand. "Don't come yet. I'm not sure you learned your lesson."

She panted. "Oh ... God... Derek, what the fuck is that thing? It puts Buzz to shame."

"So then you approve?" I slipped two fingers inside her sopping hole, rocking her gently.

"I do. Mmm .... it's like the Viking of vibrators."

Gripping her hips, I peppered her taut abdomen with kisses. Watching her arousal only fueled mine. I was desperate to be inside her pussy or her mouth. My cock was rock hard and ached for relief. "Do you want more? More of the Viking of vibrators."

"Yes ... oh ... please. I want the Viking. And I won't come until you tell me it's okay."

"That's my good girl."

I grabbed up the Viking, as Nia now called it, and kept it on its lowest setting. I continually pressed it into her velvety wetness and took it away right before she came. Her gorgeous as fuck body thrashed on the bed while I jacked myself slowly. She was such a good girl for me. She didn't ask or beg once for me to let her come. My baby took her delicious torment and waited patiently.

Finally, neither one of us could take it a second longer. *God Damn.* I was so turned on watching her firmly sculpted body tense in delirious longing, I could have shot my cum on the carpet. Instead, I let go of my cock. She was about to have a monstrous release, and it was all hands and fingers on deck.

I sealed the Viking on her clit, and thrust two digits deeps inside, no longer holding back. Her body shuddered, trying to hang on.

"Now, baby. Now you can come."

I clicked it to the highest setting, and she unraveled like never before.

"That's it, baby. You squirt for me."

Her cum blasted forth in torrential sheets, dousing me and the floor in a current of her juices.

"Good girl. Give me all your cum."

Nia's pleasure screams shook the walls while she continued to squirt like a violent rainstorm. She was never sexier than in the throws of a climax of this proportion. She was beautiful. She was mine.

While her wrung out body, slick with sweat, recovered from her mammoth orgasm. I tossed aside the Viking and petted her spent pussy.

"Oh, Derek," she whimpered in a hushed barely audible voice. "That was... It was... Fuck..."

I pressed my lips to her smooth mound. "You were incredible, my angel. The way you held back until you were given permission to come. I've always said good things happen to those who wait."

She exhaled. "You were right. All hail the Viking."

My mouth led a trail of kisses up her stomach, to her rounded breasts. Fuck, how I loved her perky tits. They were so reactive to the touch. Her nipples always appeared permanently at attention, like two pieces of hard candy, asking to be pinched, sucked, and occasionally bitten.

I continued my exploration to her neck and nuzzled on that spot that drove her crazy. She was still tied up and blindfolded. The expression on her lips was one of pure bliss.

"Mmm...if you're trying to make me horny again, Mr. Pierce, keep it up."

"Do you think you deserve what's coming?"

In between heavy breaths she said. "Yes. Please. I want it."

I maneuvered myself until I was straddling her face. I had never fucked her mouth in this position, and couldn't wait to give it to her, rougher than ever. I'd been a walking hard-on since I saw her in that green dress at the wedding.

My cock stretched to even greater fullness as my tip rested on Nia's chin. "Oh, you're going to get it, baby. Now go on, take me in your mouth like a good girl."

Nia's lips upturned in a sinful smirk. She loved to suck cock. She was also fucking unbelievable at it.

Her tongue twirled around my shiny dome. "I definitely want what's coming. I want you to shoot your cum down the back of my throat."

Jesus! She said that like a bona fide porn star—and I was about to fuck her face like one. She opened her willing mouth wide for me, and I slowly pushed my length inside. "That's it. Get me nice and wet, angel."

She coated me in her saliva as I rocked in and out with easy strokes. Watching the way her lips snaked around my shaft, under my total control, fueled my need to be buried in the back of her throat. I ramped up my thrusts while her suction power increased. *Yes, my angel, you suck it.*

I gripped the headboard and plunged deeper inside. "Fuck ... yes... Take it all."

Once I was lodged in her throaty folds, I pumped sharp and quick and released her. As I extracted my cock, strings of spit splashed on Nia's face.

I wiped her clean with my hand. "Are you okay? I'm trying my best not to be too rough with you. It's not like you can use your safe word when your mouth is full."

"Honey, I'm fine. I'm better than fine. You've got me all worked up again. I just have one request, well two."

I grasped my dick, and lightly stroked it. "What's that, sweetie?"

"Could you take off the blindfold?"

"Of course." I removed the blindfold and flung it aside. "There's my girl. What else?"

Her long eyes lashes fluttered. "Could you also untie one hand, in case I want to..."

I perched my veiny girth on her bottom lip. "Touch yourself?"

Her breath washed over my erection. "Yes. You know sucking your cock turns me on."

I released her left wrist. "You're such a naughty little thing, aren't you?"

"What can I tell you?" She teased my tip with her tongue and peered up at me. "You married a bad lady."

"I'm so glad I did. I love you, Nia."

"I love you too," she whispered, and then with a glint in her eyes said, "Now fuck my face the way God and nature intended."

I bent down and kissed her forehead. "Whatever my girl wants. Just promise me, if it's too much, hit the bed three times with your hand because I'm not holding back. Understand."

"I understand."

I slid myself back into her soft, sweet mouth. Damn, she was so fucking good. I settled into fuller thrusts, as she gradually took in more inches. Her muffled groans sounded like she was enjoying her meal of cock. And this was just the first course.

I pulled out to my tip. Nia knew exactly what I wanted. She slithered her tongue around the ridge of my head, causing my balls to contract. Drops of pre-cum followed.

"Mmm … may I have it?" she begged. "It's so creamy and delicious."

"Yes, baby. It's just a small taste of what's coming."

She gulped my crown inside, and slipped her left arm between us so she could touch herself. Her pretty mouth opened up for me and I fed her more of my hardness. We both moaned under the dual pleasure Nia provided us. This was one messy blowjob. Her drool overflowed, ran down her chin, and once again my ironclad cock shined with a fresh coat of saliva. I was giving her a thorough face reaming, and she loved every single second of it.

I released her, so she could catch her breath. I clasped my lubricated shaft, stroked myself and heaved. "Is my girl, still okay?"

"Yes. Oh … God… Can I come again? I'm getting … ah … I'm close."

"Yes… Oh fuck … you can come."

She opened her mouth like a hungry baby bird and tongued my balls. *Jesus, the things this woman did to me.* She had a way of turning me into a primal beast. I shoved my swollen sac inside, and her cheeks bulged. I ground on her face, and my hand worked my cock into a raging fury. I was nearing the brink. And from the sounds of Nia's slightly muted passion cries, so was she.

With my other hand bracing myself against the headboard I drew my balls out of her succulent cavern, and our eyes met. "Are you ready for my cum, baby?"

"Yes ... give it to me."

My fingers laced around the back of her head, holding her in place. My pulsating, granite-like phallus pushed past her lips and found its way to the back of her throat. She took in a huge breath and her larynx expanded to accommodate my tonsil thrashing cock. Slowly she gobbled down every last inch of me, until her lips were flat to my base.

"Jesus... Yes... Just like that..."

My grip intensified on the back of her head. I held her steady and firm while I gave her a series of throat punishing fuck thrusts.

When my balls tightened beyond the point of no return, I unleashed a massive wad, deep into her throat. I kept pumping her until I was fully drained. She gagged, but the muscles in her slippery passageway contracted and swallowed most of my seed.

I eased her head back on the pillow, and slowly pulled out of her sweet, satisfying mouth. Of course, she was covered in saliva and a little cum spilled out of the corners of her mouth, but my girl never looked hotter in her life.

"Sweetie, you're such a good girl. That was amazing."

She caught her breath, and smiled with pride. "I know, right. I'm totally awesome."

I kissed the bridge of her nose and climbed off her. "Awesome, doesn't do you justice." I freed her from the restraints. "Would you like me to hold you in the tub before bed, or I can just clean you up if you're tired."

She sat up, rubbing her wrists. "How about a bath and a glass of champagne. It'll knock my ass right out."

"That sounds like a plan."

"Oh. You said plan. Are you trying to turn me on and activate my launch sequence again?"

"Young lady, I'm starting to think a stiff wind could activate your launch sequence."

She outstretched her arms to me. "Only you can do that to me."

"Good." I picked her up, cradled her in my arms, and carried her to the bathroom. "Let's get you in the tub first. Then, I'll go down and check on Molly, and get us some champagne."

She cuddled against my chest. "That's perfect."

I sat her bare butt on a towel between the two sinks and drew her a bath. "You relax, angel. I'll be right back." I grabbed my robe and headed out.

When I got down to the kitchen, our black lab mix, Molly scampered off the couch and ran to me with her tail going a mile a minute. "Hey, does someone want a treat?"

Molly acted like she understood me and stared at the treat jar with laser focus. Turns out, I could never say no to her either. Both of my girls were spoiled, but I wouldn't want it any other way. All forty pounds of her sat intently while I fished out a treat and tossed it to her. She snatched it out of the air and crunched it up.

I checked both of our phones on the kitchen island. Nia's was dead. *Damn it.* Her and her phone. Every time I thought she became a little more responsible with it, I'd find it dead, turned off, or lying on the seat of the car. I tucked it in the pocket of my robe and grabbed my cell. *Oh, fuck.* Another text from Madison's stunt double, Ali, was waiting for me. I should have never told Keith it was okay to give everyone filming on location in Japan my number. At the time, I remembered how frustrated I used to get as an actor, wanting to deal with the producer directly and not an assistant. I always vowed if I ran the show, I would be more hands on, make the actors and crew feel like they weren't just hired guns. I assumed everyone would only contact me if it were an emergency.

I tapped on the text. It was a picture of the jagged cliff at the Sanin Kaigan National Park in Japan that Ali was due to jump off of, in Madison's place. It was the cliffhanger and money shot for the season finale of *The Alec Stone Chronicles.* Getting the permits to film there was a nightmare, but it would be worth it.

If Ali Cameron hadn't looked identical to Madison, my co-star, I would have fired her long ago. She had bedded half the crew and had started sleeping her way through the cast, which caused unnecessary drama on set. I was always professional, yet distant with her. I wasn't about to have another Mandy Hamilton situation on my hands. My marriage to Nia was too important to risk a misconstrued interaction. Better for her to think I was a dick than for her to think she had a shot in hell with me. I even considered green screening the shot instead of going on location, just to avoid this. But then I changed my mind. Doing the shot in Japan would be the perfect way to end the first season of *The Alec Stone Chronicles.* As a producer and star of the show, it was a chance for me to make my mark.

As with all of Ali's texts, I didn't respond and deleted the message. Then, I poured the champagne, and went upstairs, with Molly tagging along.

"Hey, what took you so long?" Nia asked. She looked adorable in the bath, with her dark hair piled on top of her head.

I handed her the champagne and hung up my robe.

"Wow! Either you missed me in the last five minutes, or you were hankering for the *Veuve Clicquot.*" I settled in behind with her back to my front, and she let out a little sneeze. "Hey. Are you okay? I hope you're not getting sick. Maybe the champagne is a bad idea?"

She snatched up her glass. "I'm fine. I think I'm just tired from the wedding and the rehearsal dinner last night. But, it was great, wasn't it? Brooke and Tom looked so happy."

I scooped up some bubbles, running them over her stomach and breasts. "Yes. They did."

"I just wish Steve and Scott could've come."

"I do too. But they are coming to visit for a week in January. And don't forget, I'm flying Aunt Mary Jane and Uncle Bill out here for New Year's Eve. My parents are coming too."

"I know. You're so good to me, my sexy, hot husband." She pressed her lips to my cheek.

"Hang onto to that thought, young lady, because I need to scold you."

She turned with a jolt. "About what? Am I in trouble?"

"Yes. Your phone. It's dead."

"Oh. Well. I mean it's late. You and I are together. If anyone really needed to get in touch with me, they could call you."

"So, now I'm your answering service?"

She shot me that irresistible smile. "Could you be? Because that would be totally awesome. Were there any calls for Mrs. Nia Pierce?"

"You think you're hilarious, don't you?"

"Well, duh." She giggled. "But, seriously, did you get any messages? Anyone trying to track me down?"

"Um … no. My phone was silent." I wrapped her up in my arms and held her tight, pushing Ali's text out of my mind.

"So, see. It's all good." She sneezed again. "I'm fine. It's just the bubbles."

"Just to be safe, I'd better get you to bed."

"But I'm not done with my champagne. Besides, we didn't even discuss the most important thing ever."

I gave into her and we both sipped our *Veuve Clicquot*. "There's a most important thing ever?"

"Of course. Adam's Maxwell's invite to The Purple Peacock. How soon can we go?"

"You really want to do that?"

"Oh God, yes! I want to experience everything. I want to experience it with you."

"And with us, there is no limit to the pleasures we can share, all except one. I drew the line in the sand about something with Adam tonight."

She peered up at me with her innocent looking doe eyes. "I don't understand."

"Adam asked me a question he considers common in the BDSM lifestyle. He asked if I was interested in sharing you with him. I told him flat out, no."

She cocked her head. "Like a three-way?"

"Yes. You would be with both of us at the same time."

She looked as if her imagination was running wild. "So, I'd have a dick in my pussy, and in my butt? Or one in my mouth, while the other one is taking me from behind? That's a whole lot of cock to think about."

"Start thinking about this. It's not going to happen."

"Oh, come on. Can't I envision it for just a second? Your eyes practically popped right out their sockets when I told you Christa wanted to have a three-way with us."

I teased. "Ah, yes. The curvy one."

She splashed me. "See. You're probably still thinking about it. I guess it's nice to know we're wanted. We're totally three-way worthy."

"Is that something you want to seriously explore?"

"No. Why? Do you?"

"Come here." She settled back into my arms. "I would never want to deprive you of anything you wanted to experience, and yet when Adam asked about sharing you, I wanted to punch him. The thought of another man laying his hands on you makes my blood boil."

She ran her fingertips over my chest. "That's kind of hot, Mr. Pierce."

I kissed the top of her head. "You're kind of hot, Mrs. Pierce. I still don't think you realize how sexy you are. Adam was quite taken with you."

"Well, Adam can't have me." She lifted her head to meet my gaze. "I'm yours. I've felt like that since the first night we were together."

"I felt that way too. You are mine, and I am yours. We belong together."

"Please don't ever let go."

"Never." I leaned in to kiss her, and she suppressed the tiniest high-pitched sneeze.

"I'm sorry. I ruined the moment. Kiss me."

"Let's get you to bed. I'm afraid sneezes are like baseball. Three sneezes and you're out of the tub. Come on, angel."

"But, we haven't finished our champagne yet."

"I'm afraid I have to insist."

Nia relented. We dried off and climbed in bed. She was tucked into her usual spot, with my arms folded around her. It was going to be near impossible falling asleep in Japan without her head resting on my chest, and kissing her goodnight. What she said at the wedding tonight about being apart for ten days weighed on me as well. We were better together than apart. The pressure of producing and starring in *The Alec Stone Chronicles* was stressful, but shooting in Vegas and being able to come home and see my wife every day kept things in check. Just one look at my girl's beautiful face, so happy to see me, kept the pressure from spinning out of control. Our lives were balanced, and happy. Marrying her was the best decision I ever made.

"Derek. You better kiss me goodnight. I'm more tired than I thought. I'm about to fall asleep."

"Of course, baby." I pressed my lips to hers and brushed the back of my hand over her cheek. "You feel warm. Are you sure you're okay?"

"I'm just sleepy." She yawned. "I hope you don't mind, I'll be camped out on top of you. Molly took my spot."

Molly lifted her head at the mention of her name then made a little nest, taking up even more space.

"I don't mind at all. Goodnight, my sweet girl, I love you."

Chapter Two

"Hey, good morning, beautiful."

Just as predicted, Nia didn't budge all night. But something wasn't right. She usually woke up full of energy, ready to tackle the day. Now, I could barely rouse her.

I gently lifted her off me. "Sweetie. Can you hear me?"

She groaned with displeasure and rolled over. "It's so hot in here. Oh … my head."

"Did the champagne give you a headache?"

"I don't know."

I touched the palm of my hand to her forehead. "Baby, you're burning up. I had a feeling you were going to get sick. Maybe I should take you to Quick Care to see a doctor."

"No. I don't need to see a doctor," she whined. "I just want to sleep."

"Okay. I'm going to go for a jog with Molly, but if you don't feel better by the time I get back, you're going to Quick Care."

She mumbled something argumentative and pulled the covers over her head.

After my run with Molly, I jumped in the shower. Nia was still fast asleep. If she needed to see a doctor, convincing her would take some doing.

I called for backup. "Julia. It's me, Derek. I hope I didn't catch you at a bad time."

"Hi. Your timing is perfect. Phillip just took Joshua and the dogs to the park. I can't believe it's seventy degrees in December."

"I know. It's nice. Molly and I just got back from a run."

"What's going on?"

"Well, I'm not a hundred percent sure, but I think Nia might need to go to Quick Care, and..."

"What happened?"

"My best guess is she has a sinus infection. She'd kill me for saying this, but she's drooling and snoring. Plus, she's running a fever."

"Oh. She probably just needs an antibiotic."

"That's what I'm thinking too, but you know how she is."

"Yup. She can be really stubborn. What's your plan?"

"I'm down in the kitchen making her some toast. If she's doesn't rally in an hour, do you think you could help me out? I just don't want to take any chances since I'm leaving town soon."

"Sure. Phillip will be out for a while. I can come over if she gives you a hard time. Heck, I'll drag her ass there, if you need me to. It's been a long time since we threw down. I'm up for the challenge."

I chuckled because Julia had a magic way with Nia. They were like sisters. When we broke up, I knew the only way I'd get Nia to hear me out was if I enlisted Julia to help me. She and I saw eye to eye on many things, much to my wife's chagrin.

"I can always count on you. Thanks, Julia. I'll text you in an hour and let you know."

"Sounds good. Oh, and don't worry about her when you're gone. We aren't headed to California, until the twenty-third. You're coming back on the twenty-first, right?"

"Yeah. I should get in late on the twenty-first. It's been a while since we've been apart like this ... so, I appreciate it."

"No problem. I've got your back."

"You always have. Thank you. I'll text you in a bit."

I fixed Nia a tray with juice, toast, and a bottle of water, and carried it to the bedroom with Molly leading the way. Our dog burst through the door first and jumped on the bed.

"*Molly*," Nia croaked out. "Lay down." She immediately spun in a circle and curled up under her arm.

"How are feeling, baby?" I placed the tray next to her on the bed. "Can you eat something for me?"

"I'm not very hungry."

"Just a couple of bites, angel. I have some juice for you too."

"If I do, can I go back to sleep?"

"We'll see. Come on, now. Sit up."

She hoisted herself up, and rubbed her hands over her face. "I must look a mess."

"Of course not," I lied. She was my sick little mess with a drippy nose. I handed her some tissues. "Here. You have a little, something."

She touched her nose with one hand and grabbed the tissues with the other. "Oh good God. I'm disgusting."

"You're not disgusting. But, I think you might need to see a doctor."

"Well, I can't go to Quick Care. There are sick people there. I'm sure it's just a twenty-four-hour bug or something."

"Just, eat a little toast, and if you feel better, then you're probably right. But if you don't…"

She plucked up the toast. "I'm eating."

"Good girl."

My phone vibrated in my pocket. Shit, it was Ali. I rejected the call.

"Is that Keith?" she asked.

"Yeah. It's Keith. I'll call him back later."

"Tell him to never mention seeing my unmentionables last night."

"I'll let him know." What the fuck was I doing? Now, I felt sick. My stomach knotted and churned. I couldn't keep this from her, and risk everything. I had to tell her the truth. "Nia, I need to tell you something."

"Okay," she said as she fed a piece of toast to Molly, and put the rest of it on her plate.

I took her hands in mine. "The truth is, that wasn't Keith who called. I just lied to you. I'm sorry."

A look of shock swept across her face as my confession sunk in. "What? Why would you do that? Who was it?"

"It was Ali Cameron, Madison's stunt double."

"Why is she calling you? How did she even get your cell number?"

"It's my fault. I told Keith to give it to everyone who's going to Japan. I had no idea she'd be calling and texting me."

"She texts you too?" She released my hands and sank down into the bed. "Now I feel even worse."

"Oh, sweetie, don't. She doesn't mean a thing to me. I haven't responded to her text messages, so maybe that's why she's calling. In all honesty, I wanted to fire her. But for the sake of the show, and the last shot of the season, I can't."

"What about for the sake of us? Is she another Mandy Hamilton?"

Nia's eyes flooded with tears. God, I hated to see her cry, especially because of me. "Sweetie. Please don't cry."

"I can't help it," she sobbed softly into her tissues.

Maybe some of her tears were because she wasn't feeling well, but my fuck ups from the past left some old demons behind. "Look... This is why I told you about Ali. I thought I could just ignore her, we'd get the shots we needed in Japan, and then not renew her contract. But, you have a right to know that she's been contacting me. I didn't want to keep it from you. And I'm going to take care of it."

"Are you going to fire her?"

"No. It's too late. I'm sorry. I can't do that. But, trust me. I will put a stop to her contacting me directly. Let me talk to Keith about it. We'll figure it out." Nia hung her head. "Baby. Look at me." Her glassy, weary eyes met with mine. "I won't ever jeopardize what we have. You are my everything. The day we got married, what did I vow to you?"

"That in your arms, I would always find love, and family. That I would forever be, home."

"That's right. And, in sickness and in health and when we need to go to the doctors for our drippy, plugged-up noses."

"You kind of had me in the palm of your hand until that last part."

"Oh, I did? I should've quit while I was ahead." I handed her the glass of juice. "Here, take two sips for me, and I'll let you rest while I call Keith. I'm going to fix this. I promise."

She drank a little juice and settled back onto her pillow. I gave her a quick peck on the forehand and went to my office to call Keith.

"Hey, Keith, it's me."

"I'm afraid you'll have to be more specific," Keith teased. "I was traumatized at Brooke and Tom's wedding by Nia's Downton Abbey, and I done lost my mind."

"Very funny." I laughed. "I'm afraid that's my fault. I'm the one who told her to do it. I'm starting to think the private dining room is not so private after all."

"They should rename it, the dining room of privates. Earlier we caught Sue Peterson on her knees blowing Jeff."

"And yet you ventured back in the room?"

"So ... anyway ... boss, what do you need from me?"

"Well, it's Ali. I'm afraid we might have a problem. She's been texting me, and this morning, she called."

"What is up with that trashy ho? I guess you're the only one going to Japan that she hasn't banged? She's trying to line up her entertainment."

"Even Ray?"

"Especially Ray. Your director of photography hasn't gotten laid since his divorce."

"Look, I'm not judging. God knows you could've called me that in my twenties, especially when I was on location. I really don't care who Ali fucks as long as she does her job, and quits calling me. I don't need any extra stress. I have a feeling Nia's going to have a hard time while I'm in Japan. Hell, I don't want to be away from her either."

"Well, I hate to be the one who said I told you so, but CGI is a beautiful thing. We could have shot all of this at the studio, and sent the crew to get exteriors."

"We've been over this a thousand times. The loyal fans of *The Alec Stone Chronicles* will expect an authentic season finale. At the end of every book, he tracks down the bad guys in different countries. You knew this is what I wanted to do all along. Being on location adds that extra layer of screen magic. My dad has said for years, there's nothing like it."

"You don't need to convince me. Tim and I are excited to go Japan. You want me to take care of Ali for you?"

"Could you? I've got a conference call with Dad and the other producers, and Nia's sick."

"She's sick? Probably caught a cold being half naked in the private dining room."

"That reminds me. Don't tease her about that."

"Well, that's just going to break Tim's heart. He's working up an entire routine of pussy willow type jokes."

"Buddy, I'm begging you. I'll have to pay the price. Tell Tim to save them for the plane. Everyone is flying commercial except for you, me, Jake and Tim."

"Tim does love your plane. Consider it done. He says he wasn't cut out to fly with the masses. And don't worry about Ali. I'll call her right now and tell her if she needs anything to contact me because you're spending time with your wife."

"Let's hope that does the trick. Otherwise, I will be forced to block her from my phone. Oh, and before I forget. Did you order the *Prada* sunglasses for everyone for Christmas?"

"Yeah. That's nice of you. I think everybody will appreciate it."

"Well, it's the least I could do since everyone is working at the holidays."

"I'm glad to hear you say that, because I couldn't decide between two styles so for myself, I ordered both of them. I ordered a pair for Nia too."

"I'm glad you did, on both counts. You actually just gave me an idea. Maybe I'll order Nia some things from *Prada* before I go. A little pre-holiday spoiling. Is there anything else you had your eye on? Or that you think Nia would like?"

"I can't say *Nada* to *Prada*. I did hear Nia say something about wanting boots for Christmas. You should probably get a bag to go with them. She'll want black. 'Cause black is beautiful, if I do say so myself."

"And if I order, say, a wallet for my overworked assistant that would be good too?"

"That's a Christmas bonus and a half. I guess I'll have to get you two fruitcakes."

"Just get Ali off my back, and we are even."

"You got it. Later."

While it was fresh on my mind, I fired up the computer and went to the *Prada* website. Then, I decided to buy Nia a black dress too. She should wear something new for our night at The Purple Peacock. Once those purchases were done, I couldn't resist clicking on our favorite kink site. Yes, there it was, the perfect thing to adorn Nia's hot little ass underneath the black velvet dress I ordered her from *Saks*. Just thinking about it, made my cock swell. I would plan a night for her she would never forget.

A loud sneeze sounded from the bedroom. It was time to text Julia. Nia was going to see a Doctor, whether she liked it or not.

* * * *

"Well, hello, stubborn," Julia said as she flung the comforter off Nia. "I understand you're giving Derek a hard time about going to the doctors. Gee, that's so unlike you."

Nia covered herself back up. "Oh, fuck me! Derek, how could you rat me out to the boss?"

"It's for your own good, angel." I placed her soft, black yoga pants and hoodie on the bed. "I need you to be a good girl and get dressed. Julia is going to take you to Quick Care."

"But..." She put her head in her hands. "I don't..."

I sat on the bed. "Look at it this way. The faster you get better, the sooner I can call Adam Maxwell and arrange our evening at The Purple Peacock."

"So, you guys are going?" Julia asked, eyes wide with intrigue.

"Looks that way," I answered. "Although, if Nia doesn't get better soon, we will have to postpone until I get back from Japan."

Very slowly, Nia grabbed her hoodie and shoved it over her head. "Okay. You two win. I don't have the strength to fight both of you. I'll go to Quick Care."

Julia handed Nia her yoga pants. "Wow! That was easy. Either you must be really sick, or you really want to go to the BDSM club."

"I suppose it's a little of both. Do you and Phillip want to come with us?" Nia asked.

"I don't know. I guess I'm not in a very handcuffs and crotchless panty kind of place. I'm still breastfeeding," Julia replied. "Although, thinking back, the handcuff night was how I got pregnant in the first place."

Nia laughed a little. "Something to share with the grandchildren someday."

I kissed her little, sick head. "Sweetie, I'm going to go to the office. My conference call starts shortly."

"Okay." She pouted. "I still don't want to go."

"I know." I smoothed the hair from her face. "But, just think, when you get back, I'll order the chicken soup you like from the club. Thanks again, Julia. I owe you one."

* * * *

"I think that went well, don't you, Dad?"

"Yes. But, at the end of the second Alec Stone book, he goes to the Congo. For the sake of the budget, and being picked up for a third season, let's try to green screen what we can. CGI saves a lot of money."

Astounded, I stared at the phone for a moment. "I don't understand. You've always said there's nothing like being on location."

"Son, when I started in this business we didn't have much choice. Plus, an international shoot of this magnitude ... well, I can tell the executives from the network aren't pleased."

"Did I fuck this up?"

"No. I'm not saying that. I'm saying for a freshman show, we've taken a huge risk. There are no guarantees in this business. The network will be watching our ratings that much closer since we went over budget. If the risk in Japan pays off, we're good. I just need you to make this work."

"I won't let you down, Dad."

"I'm not doubting you. But, I speak from experience, shooting on location can be tough. I'm sorry I won't be there. It's just too close to Christmas. I have a feeling this is the last year Dina's girls will believe in Santa Claus. They're growing up so fast. Too fast for this old man's tastes."

"It seems like just yesterday Dina was pregnant with Holly. Time really flies."

"It does. Although, I'm sure it doesn't feel that way to your sister. She said it was the longest nine months of her life. Speaking of being pregnant, how's my daughter-in-law? Any chance, I'm going to have a new grandbaby to spoil anytime soon?"

"Boy, you don't miss an opportunity to drop a hint. Actually, Nia is sick. Her friend, Julia took her to Quick Care."

"Why didn't you take her?"

"Julia offered. Besides, we had the conference call."

"I could've handled it for you. Family first, Derek. Always remember that."

Nia appeared in the doorway with slumped shoulders and a pouty lip. "Speaking of family. My girl is back. I need to take care of her."

"Okay, we'll touch base before you leave for Japan. Tell Nia I hope she feels better."

"Will do. Bye, Dad."

"Derek, guess what?" Nia asked. "I'm sick. I have a sinus infection."

"Really? That's shocking," I teased and went to her side. "Did you get a prescription for an antibiotic?"

"Yes." She handed it to me. "Julia was going to fill it, but Phillip called her. Joshua was hungry and throwing a fit."

"Okay. I'll do it. Now, get into bed and let me take care of you, angel."

* * * *

Over the next forty-eight hours, Nia stayed in bed. My poor girl got hit hard with the sinus infection and slept most of the time. Last night, she rallied a bit. She ate some soup, showered and put on the Christmas pajamas I bought her last year.

The next morning, Nia was feistier than ever. She sat up in bed, unbuttoning her pajamas.

"Young lady, what do you think you're doing? You're sick, remember?"

She ripped off her top and threw it on the floor. "I feel all better. You know how I know? I'm super horny."

"Well, in that case, get those bottoms off too. It feels like forever since I've been inside you." I stripped off my boxers.

"Yes, sir." She gleefully got naked for me. "Looks like I'm not the only horny one. According to your alarm cock, it's high noon."

She was right. My cock was already hard, and as anxious to fuck her as I was. I quickly whipped a toy down the hallway, Molly ran after it, and I shut the door.

Returning to the bed, I found Nia brushing her fingertips over her pebbling nipples. Her body appeared to ripple with need. "Come here." I sat on the bed and she straddled me.

She grasped my dick, and teased the tip, sliding it over her wetness. "Are you ready, husband? I feel like fucking you. I'm going to ride you ... like a horsey." She cracked up a little. "Oh my God, that was so much sexier in my head."

As I often had to do with my beautiful girl, I bit the side of my mouth to keep from laughing. She was so funny, sometimes without trying to be. She was adorable—and all mine.

"It was very sexy." I gripped her hips. "Giddy up, angel. Show me what you got."

She licked her lips. Her eyes were laced with heat, and focused on mine, just like I taught her. She guided my brick-like column into her slippery hole with a soft moan. There was nothing like the first sound she made when I slid inside her tight pussy. The way she opened up for me welcoming my cock with her slick walls full of aching lust. It was like slicing into a warm, juicy peach, each and every time.

She burrowed down on me, taking me in deep, with her fingernails digging into my shoulders. "Mmm... You feel so good." She rocked up and down, shafting my dick with a look of fiery pleasure. She was practically purring as her grinding efforts amped up to a more rigorous pace.

I slapped her ass and she squealed while her cunt drenched my cock. "That's it, baby. You ride me."

"Yes... Oh...God... Yes!" she cried, fucking me with her tits bouncing. She worked both of us into a frenzy of fuck-lust. Her soaked pussy engulfed me further inside, while her juices dripped down her thighs and coated my balls.

Jesus! I grabbed her wrists, yanking her to me and flattening onto my back. I took her mouth and ravished her like a hungry savage. Her long locks fell over my face, and I swept them up, holding them tight to the back of her head. Bending my knees, with my feet pressed into the bed, I pumped her hard and fast.

"Who's in control now, baby?"

"You are." She panted. "Ah ... oh fuck..."

I pulled on her hair, and clapped my hand to her perfect rump. "That's right. I want you to drown me in your cum."

I defiled her cunt with a sequence of hammering fuck strokes. It was a full-throttle thrashing with her completely at my cock's mercy. I steadied her hips firmly in place while I continued to pound her senseless. She gripped the comforter and surrendered to each pummeling thrust with her eyes blazing intently on mine. Without warning, she broke apart and came all over my dick. Then her quivering pussy walls made my balls clench, and I burst inside her, filling her with my cream.

I held her flush against me until our spasms subsided. "You're so amazing, angel." I kissed the top of her head. "I'm so glad you're feeling better."

"I'm feeling more than better." She sat upright, circling her hips. "I want to do it again. Please, sir, can I have some more?"

"You want more? Hmm ... that was very Oliver Twist of you."

"More like, Oliver Twisted." She grinned full of devilment, and my cock swelled anew inside her.

Still I teased, "I'm not sure if you should have more. You haven't been well."

"Oh, come on. Don't be a Scrooge."

With my stiffening erection swimming in a sea of cum soup, I swiftly moved her on her back, taking her again. "I think you just put the dick into Dickens."

She smiled, arching her back, meeting my slow, sensual strokes. "As long as you keep putting your dick into me, I'm good."

We spent the entire day in bed. I must have come inside her six or seven times. I guess you could say, I fucked the Dickens out of her.

Chapter Three

Nia looked at the packages on the bed with excitement. "Derek! What is all this? Christmas is still weeks away."

Tonight was our kinky outing at The Purple Peacock. I was leaving for Japan in a couple of days, so I wanted to spoil her, and make this evening special. What better way to start our adventure than with the gifts I ordered her from *Prada*?

My eyes coasted over her naked body, fresh from the shower. She was just so fucking gorgeous. The way her dark eyes sparkled lit up the room. Her smile had knocked me off my feet from day one. And the first time I touched her silky skin, I knew I would never be able to keep my hands off her. Even now as her heated gaze met mine, her nipples puckered in arousal. There had always been this magnetic force, this indescribable connection between us.

"It's a surprise. Just a little something for our night out."

"A couple of these boxes say, *Prada*. There is nothing little about that."

I pulled her close and nuzzled her neck. "Well, there's only one way to find out. Open them and see."

"I don't know where to begin."

"Here. Start with this one."

She opened the boots and gasped, "Oh, Derek. They're so hot. I love them. Thank you."

"Try them on for me."

She sat on the bed and slipped them on. They came to just below the knee, snug against her shapely calves.

I grasped her hands, so she could stand and model the black leather stunners.

Nia struck a pose. "Well, what do you think? I feel so tall. Maybe I should go to The Purple Peacock like this? Naked, except for my boots."

"I think this sexy, naked body is for my eyes only."

"I know. I was just being naughty." She bent over playfully to retrieve the other *Prada* box.

Her irresistible, curved ass was begging for a spanking. I smacked my palm against it and made her squeal. It was going to get more than a smack before the night's end.

"Just a little preview of what to expect tonight, angel."

"I'm liking where this evening is headed," she said, and opened up another package. "Oh my God. It's the *Prada* calf tote bag with purple lining. Oh, I see what you did there. We're going to The Purple Peacock, so the bag has a purple lining. You think of everything, Mr. Pierce."

"Indeed. Look a little closer, there's something inside."

"Purple towels? I don't get it."

"Well, I'm not a hundred percent sure of what we'll encounter tonight. But, I'm guessing it could be kind of a turn-on. I've always wanted to finger you until you come, in a public place. And that glorious pussy of yours has a squirting mind of its own."

"So, you're taking a page out of my book? You're being prepared, like a girl scout."

I took the bag, put it on the bed, and placed her hand on the crotch of my trousers. "Does this feel like a girl scout to you?"

"No. It feels like a sturdy oak." A devious grinned crossed her face. "Do I get my nature badge now?"

"Young lady, you'll be receiving many badges tonight."

She snaked her arms around my waist. "I want to earn a badge of dishonor. I'm yours to do with as you please, Sir."

"Hmm ... Sir? I think I like that."

"I did a little research online. That's what a submissive calls their Dominant."

I tucked a finger under her chin. "So, you're my submissive now?"

"Um ... well... I don't know if I'd be very good at it all the time." Playfulness oozed from her pores. "But, for tonight, I'd like to be your dirty little slut. Use me, Sir. However you like."

"God bless the internet and research." I clasped her chin, bringing her lips to mine. "You will be my dirty little slut tonight. Now bend over the bed and spread your cheeks for me. I have another little gift for you."

She did as instructed. "Little gift? Then, it isn't your cock."

I retrieved the lube and my new purchase from the kink site, a stainless steel jeweled butt plug. I removed it from its black, velvet drawstring pouch, showing it to Nia. "This is what I'm putting in your ass. All night long, think about me taking you there when we get home."

She released a shaky breath. "Yes, Sir."

"Good girl." I clicked open the bottle of lube, applied a generous dollop to her anus, and slid my finger inside. Nia mewled. *Fuck.* Her asshole was so tight and smooth. I couldn't wait to bury my cock in there when we returned from The Purple Peacock. "I'm going to put the plug in now, baby."

It glided in with ease, and Nia's body writhed in delight. "Oh ... it's cold."

"Does my dirty little slut like it?" I wiggled it back and forth.

"Oh, yes. Thank you, Sir."

I pressed my lips to the small of her back. "You look so fucking hot, baby. I'm hard as a rock looking at you bent over with the boots. Every time you call me, Sir, it sends a twinge to my cock." I gathered her to me. "Come here. I want you to see how sexy you are from behind."

I maneuvered her to the mirror. She turned her head and checked herself out. "Wow! I have ass bling. And it's purple."

"That's not what I'm talking about. Look at how sexy you are. Don't you see what I see?" I cupped her perfect bottom, and brushed her hair to the side. "Really look at yourself." I delivered soft kisses on her shoulder. "Tell me. What do you see?"

Her gaze lingered for a moment, and then she faced me. "I see a woman. A sexy woman that belongs to you."

I touched my lips to hers. "That's right. Good girl." I held her to my chest. "And tonight when we're out, you'll wear the new dress I bought you and nothing underneath. I want access to everything that's mine."

"Yes, Sir."

* * * *

"Are you sure this is it?" Nia asked.

"Yeah. It's the address Adam gave me. He said not to be surprised that The Purple Peacock looked like an ordinary office building from the outside."

We were right on the edge of Summerlin, in what used to be a booming shopping area. All the stores went belly-up during the recession and it was converted into an office park. There were just a handful of cars in the parking lot at ten p.m.

I placed my hand on her knee. "You ready, my dirty little slut?"

"I'm ready, Sir."

We climbed out of the car, and I escorted her to the side entrance, as instructed. Before, I could hit the button on the intercom the door opened. It was Adam.

"You made it." He offered his hand to me. "Thank you for coming."

Nia giggled nervously, and I shook his hand. "Thank you for having us."

"Please, come in. I'll lead the way."

Nia clutched my hand and peeked up at me with a naughty gleam in her eye. After tonight, she could check this off her sex bucket list.

The three of us journeyed down a dimly-lit unassuming hallway. You would never guess there was BDSM club here.

"By the way, Married Nia Pierce, you look exquisite this evening," Adam said off-handedly. Which was my thought, *Hands off my wife*.

Nia squeezed my hand. "Thank you."

We halted in front of ornate double doors. Adam gripped the handles. "This is it. Welcome to The Purple Peacock."

He flung open the doors and we stood in awe of the sight before us. There was an innocent, almost heavenly glow about the spacious room. In some ways, it seemed like a typical, sleek nightclub, but the soft purple hues beaming from the corners, and a light lilac scent gave it a celestial quality. We had entered the Garden of Eden and were about to take a bite of the apple.

The marble bar was center stage. It resembled a large four-poster bed. Thick, shiny brass poles extended to the ceiling. Dark, purple, leather loveseats surrounded it, providing intimate seating.

"Well." Adam turned to us. "What do you think?"

Nia's eyes wandered around the room with her mouth gaped open. "It's beautiful. It's not at all what I expected."

"What did you expect?" Adam asked, leaning into her slightly.

"I guess, I thought it would look like a dungeon, with rows of whips and chains ... and one of those Saint Andrew's crosses."

He arched his eyebrow quizzically. "Are you disappointed?"

Flustered, Nia responded, "Um ... no... I don't know ... I—"

He interrupted, "Because, we have a room, just like that. We have several rooms actually. There's a Playroom, Sir's Lounge, and the Master's Suite, to name a few. It's basically *Disneyland* for adults."

My girl blurted. "Maybe you should rename the club Jizz-ney-land."

Adam and I busted out laughing. That was Nia for you. Adorably hilarious and uncensored. God, I loved my angel.

"Perhaps, we should get a drink? What do you think, Derek? Is champagne okay?" I nodded in agreement, and Adam motioned for the bartender. "Patrick, a bottle of *Veuve Clicquot*, please."

When Nia sat down, she winced and altered herself about, finding a comfortable position.

It was comical watching her try to play it off, like she didn't have a butt plug in her ass. I took a seat next to her, nestling her ear. "What seems to be the trouble?"

She muttered under her breath. "No trouble. I'm adjusting the family jewels."

Adam remained standing, and the bartender set us up with drinks. There were only a few people scattered throughout the club. One couple reclined on a round bed in the far right corner. I swear they looked familiar, but I couldn't be sure from this distance. At the end of the bar, there was a woman kneeling next to a man dressed in black. She was wearing a collar and leash, and a revealing purple dress. She reminded me of Christa, the curvy fitness instructor. The gentleman stroked her long, auburn locks, and whispered into her ear. She looked so peaceful on the floor.

When we all had our champagne in hand, Adam raised a glass. "Well, here's to new experiences. Cheers." He took a sip and put his glass down. "Nia, you look like you have a million questions."

Nia ran her fingertips over the ridges of the crystal champagne flute. "I kind of do. Was it that obvious?"

"Ask me anything you like," Adam responded.

"Well, for starters, why do you call the club The Purple Peacock, and where did you get these beautiful lamps with purple feathers? Are they supposed to look like bedside lamps, since the bar looks like a bed?" My girl rambled just like she did the night we met. "Oh, and is that couple going to have sex on that bed over there? Is the lady kneeling on the floor doing it because she wants to, or because she has to? Are you really a Dom? What does that actually mean? Oh ... God... Sorry, I talk too much."

Adam smiled. "No, you don't. Derek, you have a very curious wife. Curiosity is a good thing. It keeps life interesting. So, to answer your first question, we chose a peacock, because some say the male peacocks' sexual prowess is in his train of feathers. He uses it to pick a mate."

"There aren't any purple peacocks, though, am I right?" I interjected.

"No. Not that I know of. We picked purple, because, well, the painting on the wall over there is the artist's depiction of a mythical purple peacock. It's a fantasy. And that's what we hope to do for our invited guests, fulfill a fantasy. But, and I can't stress this enough, the other reason I wanted to be a silent partner is because I wanted to see those fantasies fulfilled safely. Safe, sane, consensual, and private is our motto here. There are so many people, especially young, single women interested in the lifestyle since *Fifty Shades of Grey* put BDSM in the mainstream. There's also a lot of posers, and dangerous situations they can find themselves in if they aren't careful. That's why it's by invite only. And even then, fake Doms have slipped in here on occasion, not to mention a nosey reporter or two, looking to expose us to the masses."

"But wouldn't more exposure be great for business?" Nia asked. "The place is pretty empty."

Adam retrieved his glass. "Trust me. It's not about the money. It's about providing people a discreet, safe place to explore their fetishes, or learn about the lifestyle. Plus, only a few people were on the list tonight. I wanted you and Derek to feel comfortable. Oh, and as for the couple on the bed over there. You know them. It's Jeff and Sue Peterson. If my instincts are correct, they are contemplating whether or not to join the other couples in the Playroom. Normally, going in there means you're open to sharing."

I grimaced at the thought of someone touching Nia. "My wife and I will be skipping the Playroom. I'm keeping her all to myself."

Adam nodded. "As you wish. Not everyone shares the same kinks. BDSM is like a huge buffet, only sample what you like."

"Derek Pierce, is that you?" a male voice called from the other side of the room.

The sharply dressed couple made their way around the large bar. I knew I'd met this middle-aged man before, but I couldn't place him. The woman was a stunning, petite, blonde, with shoulder length hair.

He offered his hand. "Derek, I don't know if you and Nia remember me. I'm Doctor Parker, Lou? I was on call the night Nia was in the hospital. Gosh, it's been almost a year now."

"Yes. Of course." I stood up and we shook hands. "Nice to see you again."

"Good to see you too. And I would add, under much better circumstances. How are you, Nia?" Lou asked. "You look great."

"Compared to the last time you saw me. I'm excellent. Is this your wife?"

"Yes, forgive me." He put his arm around her. "This is my wife, Tracey."

Tracey gushed slightly. "It's brilliant to meet you both. I remember the night Lou came home and said he saw Derek Pierce at hospital. I was positively gobsmacked."

"I love your British accent," Nia said. "I could listen to you talk all day."

"That's so lovely of you to say. You'll find if you hang out here often enough, there's a few Brits and Aussies that frequent the club."

"Really? How long have you lived in Vegas?" Nia inquired.

"It's been over ten years," Tracey replied.

Lou looked at Tracey with a warm smile. "I met her on 'holiday,' as they say in London, and knew, I couldn't live without her."

Tracey chimed in, "We got married by Elvis, and this old sod cried like a baby."

"What can I say? 'Love Me Tender,' gets me every time," Lou quipped. "I'm a sentimental sap."

"I think that's great," I added. "The world could use more sentimental Elvis-loving saps."

Tracey sighed. "Oh … see. I had a feeling about you. I always used to say to Lou when we'd watch you on *First Bite*, I bet Derek Pierce is just as dashing off-screen as he is on. I was right. Now, it looks like Adam is the next eligible bachelor on the list. We should find him a nice subby to settle down with and marry."

Adam bristled. "Tracey, you're forgetting I'm not the marrying kind. Let's talk about the two of you. I reserved a private room for you this evening. I have set it up according to your specifications."

"That won't be necessary," Lou replied. "I was on call tonight, and I'm afraid I've been called in. Good thing I didn't have a drink, but then again, I never do when we come here. I wouldn't want to dull the experience for anything in the world. Having said that, whatever Nia and Derek order, please put it on my tab. Tracey is being rather stoic, but trust me, you two have made her night."

Tracey elbowed him. "Darling, stop. They'll think I'm daft."

"Not at all," I replied. "It's been a pleasure to meet you both."

She glanced up at Lou, teasing, "If I wasn't so bloody knackered, I'd stay, just to see where the evening leads. But, perhaps another time. Rain check?"

"Of course," I responded.

We exchanged good-byes and I spotted Jeff and Sue rising from the bed in the corner. I motioned for Nia to have a look.

"No way," she exclaimed. "Adam, are they going into the direction of the Playroom?"

"It looks that way," he said. "They have really started to embrace the lifestyle. Normally, I wouldn't divulge that, what happens at the club stays at the club, but as you know, Sue is an open book. I'm not telling you anything, she wouldn't tell you herself."

"So totally true. You just wait until the next time I see her. I'm going to grill her like a hot dog on the Fourth of July."

The man dressed in black approached. "Sorry to interrupt, mate. I need to go over a few things before I help set up for the scene in the Master's Suite."

"No worries," Adam said. "Nia and Derek, this is my associate, Sebastian."

Sebastian was mid-thirties, like Adam and I, with a medium, solid frame, military crew cut, and distinct Australian accent. After the introductions, Sebastian got down to business.

"So, if I could talk privately for a moment. We've had a request, for some playtime."

"Sebastian, feel free to speak in front of Nia and Derek. They signed the confidentiality agreement, and Nia's very curious about the club and the BDSM lifestyle. This might answer some of her questions. If that's okay with you, Derek?"

Nia gave me one of those looks that said, "Please."

"That's fine with me."

Sebastian took out his phone and scrolled. "Well, Kristi Callender was at the munch last week. She'd like an experience with a Dom, just light BDSM, nothing too heavy. It would be her first time. Naturally, I thought of you."

Nia rested her hand on her chin. "Oh wow! So many questions. I'm almost afraid to ask. What's a munch?"

"A munch, is gathering of people in the BDSM community and people that are curious, like yourself," Adam explained. "We host them here about once a month, on Saturday afternoons. The bar and the private rooms aren't open. It's strictly to meet, socialize, and ask questions. It also helps Sebastian vet those that are interested in an invite to the club."

Nia said in astonishment, "Okay. That is so the opposite of what I thought you were going to say. Then, my next question is, are you guys like a BDSM dating service?"

"Not exactly, little lady," Sebastian answered. "But, in my opinion, we are a might safer than meeting a potential Dom online. We've made a few matches here and there. Some prefer to test the waters with an experienced Dom, and if they ask us for help, we try to give it to them. Single women are an easy target for a fake. We've heard the stories. As a Dom, it's one of the reasons I got involved. Safe, sane, consensual, and private."

"I respect that," I commented. "Adam mentioned that was your motto, and it's a good one."

"Thanks, mate," Sebastian replied. "I sure do miss your show *First Bite*. The third season was brill. I had a sub at the time, Tessa. She was a big fan. It made her so horny, every Sunday night was playtime."

"Thank you." I winked at Nia. "I get that a lot."

"What are you getting up to these days?" Sebastian asked.

"*The Alec Stone Chronicles* airs in February."

"Nice. I'll be watching." He turned his attention back to Adam. "I've got to dash off. I was wondering if you could help me with Helen. She'll be right, but for now, I think she needs us."

Nia glanced to the woman kneeling on the floor with the leash and collar. "Is Helen your girl? I mean, submissive?"

"No. I'm single at the moment," Sebastian replied. "Helen is our dear friend. She and her Dom have parted ways. It's for the best. They wanted different things.

But, she's struggling. She misses the lifestyle, and being disciplined."

"I will be there for her tonight. Whatever she needs," Adam said. "Helen, come, my pet."

While Helen crawled across the floor to Adam, Sebastian made his exit, saying he might see us shortly. I wasn't sure what he meant.

However, seeing this lifestyle up close intrigued me. Just observing Nia's reaction to everything, made me desire her even more. She was so full of surprises, so open to new, decadent experiences, so completely mine.

Adam bent down, to be eye level with Helen. "Would you like to go to the Master's Suite and watch a scene with me?"

Helen nodded. "Yes, Sir."

He stood and smoothed her hair. "Go there and wait for me. Get in your comfort pose if you like. And if you're a good girl, I'll allow you to come tonight."

Helen crawled away, with a look of contentment on her face.

I leaned against the bar. "Can I ask, is it normal for a Dom to step into another Dom's place after a breakup?"

Adam shrugged. "Who can say? I really don't know. But, I can tell you Helen has worked for us since we opened. We hired her as a cocktail waitress, and then one day she shows up to work having painted the purple peacock. She's an amazing artist. She designed the interiors of the Master's Suite and the other rooms. She's like family, and we look out for each other. If this is what she needs right now, then I'm happy to help her through it. She's one of the strongest, most creative women I know."

"That's, like awesome on so many levels," Nia said. "Tonight has been so incredible already. And, I've only had a few sips of champagne."

Adam smiled. "Well, that brings me to a question for the two of you. You're welcome to stay at the bar and finish the champagne, or you could spend some time in one of our private rooms, or if you like to watch, Jack and Emma Valentine will be in the Master's Suite this evening, performing a scene."

"What's a scene?" Nia asked with excitement in her voice.

"A scene is like a demonstration. It's a chance to watch a couple at play," Adam answered. "Jack and Emma aren't Dominant and submissive, they have more of a twenty-four-seven, master and slave relationship. They're also married and have been in the lifestyle a very long time. I asked them because their connection is so deep and genuine. The way Emma gives herself to Jack is an incredible thing to see."

I pressed my lips to Nia's temple. "Whatever you want to do, my sweet girl. It's up to you."

A huge wicked grin split her face. "Screw the champagne, I want to watch."

* * * *

"How's the plug, baby?" I whispered in Nia's ear. "Are you all right?"

Before we fully settled into the new surroundings in the Master's Suite, I needed to make sure my girl was comfortable.

"It's actually starting to hurt a little, and not in a good way." She glimpsed up at me with pleading eyes.

I kissed her forehead. "Okay, sweetie. I'll come with you to the bathroom."

"I can go by myself."

"I insist... And don't even think about arguing with me."

"I wouldn't dream of it ... Sir."

"Good girl." Adam was on the other side of the room with Helen. "Adam, I'm going to take Nia to the restroom. Can you point me in the right direction?"

"Lisa is right outside the door. She'll show you the way."

Lisa, who I assumed was a cocktail waitress or perhaps potential participant in the evening's scene, escorted us to a special couple's bathroom. Damn, Adam thought of everything. Lisa was sweet and very attentive. She offered to get us a drink and to accompany us into the restroom. I had her wait outside.

"Bend over the sink for me, angel. Let me see."

She was eager to please. "Yes, Sir."

I pulled her dress up, exposing her gorgeous ass flesh, and palmed her perfectly sculpted cheeks. "Hmm ... so beautiful. God, I'd like to take your ass right here."

She whimpered, "Oh ... whatever Sir wants. Use me."

I dipped a finger into her wetness. "I love the effect this place has on you. You're so obedient and so fucking wet."

"Mmm ... ah... I love it too. I just want to please you."

"You do, baby. And you're going to get to come while we're here. I want everyone to see that I own all your orgasms. They are mine, and your body is mine. I'm not sharing, ever."

"I'm all yours. My body, mind, and soul belong to you."

"That's a good girl." I retreated my finger from her clutching hole. "Now spread your cheeks for me." She did without hesitation, submitting to me, opening herself up in complete abandonment. Her fingers curved about her rounded, fine ass, awaiting instruction. "Very nice. I'm proud of you for wearing this as long as you did."

"I wanted to, so I could be ready for you later. I was hoping I could have it in all night and…"

"And what, angel? Tell me."

"I wanted to see what a spanking would feel like with it inside me."

"Then, hang onto the sink. Well behaved girls get spankings too."

She gripped the edge of the counter and hunkered down on the marble. "Yes. Please."

I pressed my hand into her back, shoring her in place. Then my other hand landed on her right buttock with a crack. Quickly, I smacked the other cheek, and my cock stirred taking in the sight of her toned, enticing body quaking in pleasure. My girl loved to be spanked, the harder, the better. As I continued clapping my palm to her reddening bottom, her juices of ecstasy trickled down her thighs.

Nia's sweet cries echoed in the bathroom. "Ah … oh God … oh… Yes … more, please."

I stopped. Not because she asked for more, but because I was about to fuck her right here, and I wanted to wait. I mustered all my restraint. I would keep my edge and pump her ass fully when we got home.

"There, all done." I kissed each cheek and extracted the jeweled plug, pushing my finger inside her squinting entrance. "You're nice and open for me. I can't wait to get you home."

"Derek, please. I'm so close. Can I come now?"

I washed my hands and the plug, loving the sight of Nia reduced to a pile of aching need. "Not yet, baby.

But soon." I spotted a purple basket with washcloths. Once I dried my hands and dropped Nia's butt bling in my pocket, I cleansed her, and pulled her dress down. "We better get back out there. I don't want to keep them waiting."

She stood upright, a little wobbly in her new boots. "But, you're keeping me waiting?"

I tucked my finger under her chin. "That's right. And why is that?"

"Because, I'm your dirty little slut, and you're in charge."

"Good girl."

Lisa showed us back to the Master's Suite. She inched inside the room and looked to Adam. He shook his head "no" and she retreated to the hallway with her head down.

This room was more in line with my expectations. The exposed brick walls and tiled floor complemented two large black leather couches. It retained its trademark soft purple lighting and faint lavender scent, but the rows of paddles, floggers, and crops on the walls were in stark contrast to the bar area of the club.

Adam sat at one end of the sofa with Helen in the fetal position at his feet. A black and red padded, vertical bench was center stage. I assumed the added extensions in the shape of an X were for limbs to be restrained, spread eagle.

"Welcome back to the Master's Suite," Adam said. "I trust you found our facilities satisfying?"

Nia glared at me. "Lovely, yes. Satisfying ... well ... not yet."

Adam covered his mouth with his hand and concealed a chuckle. "I see. Hmm ... you know what they say, good things come to those who wait."

Nia threw her hands up in the air. "Oh, for the love of God. Did Derek tell you to say that?"

He laughed. "No. But, Married Nia Pierce, even if you two don't call yourself Dom and submissive, it seems to be a dynamic of your relationship. I'll let you in on a little secret. Dom's love two things. We love orgasms, and we love control, so naturally controlling orgasms is something we crave."

"I couldn't have said that better myself." I drew Nia close. "She's a greedy little thing, Adam."

"I don't doubt you for a second." He motioned toward the sofa he was sitting on. "Please, relax. Emma and Jack will begin shortly. If you have any questions during their scene, feel free to ask, but quietly. If Emma is in subspace, I don't want her disturbed."

Nia and I got comfortable next to Adam. I purposely positioned myself between them.

She asked, "What's subspace?"

Adam reached down and stroked Helen's back. "It's an altered state a submissive can experience during play. The pain and pleasure combined can trigger an endorphin rush so extreme, some of my subs said they feel like it's an out of body experience, sort of like they're floating."

"I've felt that before," Nia said. "Probably not as deep as your friend, Emma, but I understand what you mean."

"Excellent. Then, you'll understand, when the scene is over, we need to clear out of the room and give them their privacy."

"Of course," I replied. "Anything else we should know?"

Adam undid the buttons around his wrists and rolled up his sleeves. "Well, under these unusual circumstances, no."

"What unusual circumstances?" Nia asked.

"Derek being a celebrity," Adam answered. "The truth is Emma and Jack don't normally use their real names when they're here. But they're trusting you, just as you're trusting them. So, enjoy yourselves. However you like."

"Thank you, I'm sure we will." I kissed Nia's forehead.

She whispered, "We're definitely going to need those towels."

The door swung open, and Jack and Emma entered. Jack strode into the room with a confident gait. He appeared to be mid-forties, with grayish brown hair, and a muscular build. Emma's naked, supple form crawled behind him, sporting a collar and leash. She had lovely long blonde hair and porcelain skin.

Jack tugged on her leash as they made their way to the sofa. Adam stood to greet them, and I followed suit.

Jack extended his hand to Adam and then to me. "Adam, thank you for including us this evening. It's an honor to meet you, Mr. Pierce."

"Please. Call me, Derek. This is my wife, Nia."

Awe, wonder, and her mouth overtook my girl. "Hi. It's so naked to meet you. Oh ... God! I mean nice! It's so nice to meet you naked. Oh ... fuck. I'm so sorry."

Jack grinned. "It's quite all right. My Emma knows she's naked. Don't you, dear one? You may speak."

She raised her head. "I'm naked for my master."

The back of Jack's hand grazed against her cheek. "And you look beautiful, my slave."

Emma was a beautiful woman. Her hazel eyes somehow exuded excitement and serenity at the same time. Even though, she was on the floor, she wasn't beneath Jack. There was a regal quality to her posture. It was obvious. She was his queen.

He led her to the padded, leather bench and patted it. She climbed up and reclined face down. Jack slipped a black silk blindfold on Emma, before opening a metal cabinet and retrieving some purple rope.

Adam moved a bit closer. "Jack is a master at rope work. I've seen him spend hours doing the most intricate Shabari. He'll probably modify things a bit, for time, but it's still compelling to witness."

Nia and I were mesmerized watching Jack tie knots and weave the rope around her limbs like an ornamental lattice. When he finished, he stood back to admire his creation. It was a work of art. I wanted to applaud.

Jack swept Emma's hair to the side, and spoke softly in her ear, before going back to the cabinet and grabbing some sort of small wheel with a handle.

Nia leaned over me, toward Adam. "What is that?"

"It's a Warburton wheel. It's for sensation play. Jack always starts with it. He says it helps Emma go deeper into the right mindset."

When Helen heard Adam say Warburton wheel, she rose from the fetal position to watch.

Jack kissed Emma's forehead and proceeded to roll the instrument over her buttocks with precision. Her cheeks quivered, and she let out a contented moan. He repeated the same motion along the crease where her butt met her thighs.

Nia squirmed next to me. "Can we get one of those?"

"Of course, baby. I'll add it to your Christmas list."

Jack spread Emma open with his fingers and lightly blew over her ass. He said in a hushed tone, "Count for me."

As he glided the wheel over her tender crack flesh, she counted in a shaky voice, and her body trembled with each stroke. When she reached ten, he stopped, and pushed two fingers inside her, treating her to a finger fuck.

Jack praised her, "Very good, dear one."

Nia, Adam, and I were so taken with the display, none of us noticed Helen fingering herself until she released murmurs of arousal.

"Helen, you're being a very bad girl," Adam admonished in a stern, quiet tone. "You were not given permission to touch yourself. Nose in the corner. Right now."

Oddly enough, Helen's lips upturned into a slight smile. "Yes, Sir."

Adam spanked her bottom twice as she crawled to the nearest corner. "You won't be allowed to come tonight. Don't even think about touching yourself again."

Meanwhile, Emma was nearing the edge. "Permission to come, Master?"

"No, slave. You haven't earned it yet." Jack removed his fingers.

From our vantage point, I could see the slickness of Emma's pussy. He must have provided her with a bit of slack in the rope because he was able to raise her hips slightly off the table.

He pried apart her outer lips and held the wheel steady with the other hand. "You can move at your own pace, dear one. I want five. Count."

Emma slowly rolled her clit over the wheel. "Ahhh ... one.... Ooooh....t–two... Mmm ... three... Oh, Master..." Her hips sunk flat to the table.

"You pulled away," Jack reprimanded. "Now, you'll have to start over. Come on, dear one, don't make me wait."

With renewed determination, Emma tipped her hips back up and quickly reached five swipes of the wheel. By her fifth, you could see the beads of sweat forming on her skin.

Jack beamed with pride as he fisted her hair, and pulled her head up. "Good girl." He brought his mouth down on hers and lavished her with commanding kisses.

I found myself aroused, and captivated by the scene. Emma's desire to please Jack was almost palpable. While Jack continued to take Emma's mouth, I drew Nia's lips to mine and kissed her deeply. My tongue met with hers, and Nia's breathy whimpers made my cock even more rigid. Out of respect for the scene, I maintained control and broke our kiss. Nia's eyes burned with passion. She exhaled, and steeled herself, giving her full attention back to Emma and Jack.

"You will be allowed to come shortly, dear one," Jack said as he went back to the cabinet.

When Nia caught a glimpse of the vibrator, she gasped, "Oh, the Viking!"

"Shh ... baby." I squeezed her leg. "We have to be quiet."

"I'm sorry, but it looks just like my magic wand. Emma is so going to be coming."

Jack plugged "the Viking" into a nearby outlet and revved it up. He held it to Emma's pussy, but placed the flat of his hand on the small of her back so he could be in charge.

Immediately she cooed in delight. He teased her turning it off and on. She never once complained but said, "Thank you, Master," every time he turned it back on.

Nia wriggled in her seat. I slid my hand up her dress and engaged in some teasing of my own. She reached into her new bag, grabbed the purple hand towels, and spread them across my lap.

Jack turned the Viking off once more, nestling the handle in the crack of her ass. He plunged two digits inside her pussy. "Don't come, just yet, dear one. I want you to taste yourself first."

He released her hole and perched his dewy fingers at her mouth. "Suck."

She opened up and took them inside as if she was working a cock.

He patted her head, reclaimed the wand, and sealed it to her clit. Jack clicked the on switch. "Now, dear one. Come for me."

Emma came on demand. Her body shook as if jolts of lightning shot through it. Her orgasm appeared to wrench her from end to end. Her cries went from pleasure to pain, and back again.

Jack turned off the wand and caressed her worked over cunt. "That's a good girl. A very good girl that needs a little more discipline for pulling away from me earlier. I'm getting my cane."

When he said 'cane' it got my attention. I quietly asked Adam. "A cane?"

"Yes." Adam leaned in and responded in a low tone. "It's not for everyone. You need to be properly trained if you're going to use one. Jack is an expert and Emma ... well, it's something she craves. She likes to have her limits pushed."

Jack swished the cane through the air, and it whistled. Before caning her ass, he spanked her multiple times to warm her up. Then he tapped her ass several times with the cane, to prepare her even further.

Jack took a readied stance. "Twelve lashes. Count."

He wielded the cane with fineness. It was as if he was a professional fencer and Emma's ass was a worthy opponent. She screamed out in agony during the first four strikes, and then it seemed to morph into more quieted, enjoyable cries. Jack never hit the same spot twice, as the welted stripes emerged on her cheeks.

When she reached twelve, Jack dropped the cane and cradled her head in his hands. He spoke to her in such a gentle tone, I couldn't hear what he said. In fact, I glanced to Adam, thinking it was our cue to leave, and give them their privacy, but Adam mouthed for us to wait.

After a short time, Emma nodded. "Yes. Fill me. Fill me, please."

Jack hurried out of the room and quickly returned with Sebastian. Before Jack could shut the door, I saw Lisa peeking in. Perhaps she hoped to take part as well.

Jack positioned himself between Emma's legs. "Sebastian and I are going to use you, like a little whore. Suck his cock good and thorough, slave. I want to hear you gag."

"Yes, Master," Emma said with a hint of a smile.

Sebastian pushed his thumb into her mouth. "That's a good little whore."

Heat emanated from Nia's body. Without exposing her to the room, I ran my hand all the way up her thighs, and over her naked pussy. She was drenched.

"Come here, baby." I gathered her onto my lap, where she put the towels.

She wiggled her ass cleft over my burgeoning hard-on. "Is that a butt plug in your pocket, or are you just happy to see me?"

"You're so naughty. You can't help yourself." I nudged her dress up around her hips so she wouldn't get it any wetter than it already was.

She slid her hand between us, gently squeezing my hardness.   "You're   the   one   with the … massive … hard … cock."

"Behave. Or I won't let you come." I grasped her wrists. "Eyes front, and hands to yourself. Watch the scene, young lady."

By this point, Sebastian and Jack were naked from the waist down, ready to fill Emma. Jack thrust inside her with a growl, grabbing her hair and lifting her chin.

Emma's willing mouth sprung open, and Sebastian eased his cock in slowly.

Adam took off his belt and undid his pants. "Helen, come."

She crawled to his side, and he bound her wrists behind her with the belt. "May I suck it, Sir?"

He cupped her chin. "Yes, you may."

Fuck! I was the only man in the room not burying my dick somewhere. Now that Sebastian and Jack were plowing Emma to a pulp in tandem, I focused all my attention on making Nia come.

I angled us away from Adam and Helen so no one would see what was mine. "Spread your legs just a little bit more, angel. I'm going to get you off, right here in front of everyone."

She parted them for me, and my fingers skated over her silky wetness.

A ragged breath escaped. "Mmm ... yes."

The pad of my thumb circled her chubby clit. "Look at you. So beautiful, so ready to come already."

"Can I?" she begged.

"Not yet. I want you to take everything in. See, how hard Sebastian and Jack are pounding Emma? I'm fucking your ass even harder when we get home."

"Oh God!" she cried.

I covered her mouth and whispered in her ear, "Shhh, be quiet, baby, and listen. Listen. Do you hear that? The sound of fucking."

The room resonated with a melody of slapping flesh, mixed with grunts and groans. Once I trounced Nia's hole with a myriad of ramming finger thrusts, she came undone all over my hand. Her orgasm kicked off a domino effect. Jack came inside Emma's pussy. Then, Sebastian growled a string of what I assumed was Aussie slang, and finally, Adam emptied himself into Helen's mouth.

The air filled with heavy, satisfied breaths and the smell of sex hit my nose. I covered up my girl and held her close. This was indeed a night she would remember forever.

Sebastian was the first to zip up. "Adam, I'll look after Helen if you want to take Derek and Nia out the back."

"Absolutely. But, Helen is not permitted to come." Adam refastened and stood. "We should leave Emma and Jack on their own."

I helped Nia up. "Of course, just lead the way."

Adam showed us to a secret door that opened directly to the parking lot, close to our car. "Well, it seems you two enjoyed yourselves. I hope you'll come back sometime."

"Are you kidding? It was a blast," Nia said. "I almost feel drunk and I barely touched my champagne."

"It does have an intoxicating effect," Adam replied. "And who knows, maybe next time, you'll perform in a scene for us, Married Nia Pierce. With Derek of course."

I coiled my arm around her waist. "For now, all of Nia's shows are private, for my eyes only." She shivered. "And I need to get her home. She just got over a sinus infection. I don't want her catching a cold in this night air."

We said goodnight to Adam and got in the car. Nia clicked on the heat. "I have a very possessive Sir."

"Yes. You have a very possessive Sir, who's been dying to fuck you all night. I hope my dirty little slut is ready to get her ass thrashed."

"Yes, Sir!"

* * * *

Fuck! The sight of Nia kneeling on the bedroom floor wearing nothing but a collar and leash caught me and my cock by surprise.

"Baby, you look so... Jesus, I don't even have any words. How long have you been waiting for me like this?"

She glanced up at me through her thick lashes. "Not very long. I hopped in the shower when you got the phone call from Japan."

I crouched down on the floor. "I'm so sorry I had to take that call. Time zones are a pain in the ass."

"It's okay. I want things to go smoothly for you. The sooner you get there, the sooner you'll be home, and it'll be our anniversary and Christmas." She leaned over and revealed a tray. "Plus, you were so distracted, you didn't even see me snatch the champagne and glasses."

"I'm not too distracted to notice this collar and leash you're wearing. It's very sexy, Very Married Nia Pierce."

"It was even sexier earlier. Molly tried to walk me."

"That's hilarious. Is that why she came running downstairs?"

"I guess so. When I saw Helen and Emma wearing theirs, I thought it was a perfect night to debut it. I bought it off that kink site we like. Who knew I was so on trend."

I curled my finger under her collar. "My trendy little slut." Pulling her lips to mine, I seized her mouth, kissing her like I owned her, because I did. She was mine. She willingly gave herself to me that very first night we were together. Her sweet submission allowed us to experience filthy, new fuck fantasies. Tonight was no exception.

When I released her, we heaved, shallow, gratified breaths into each other's mouths. She possessed that look of sexy surrender, keeping her eyes on mine.

As I stood, I retrieved the champagne and touched it to her bottom lip. We were so in sync. She knew exactly what was in my dirty mind. I tipped the bottle, and she drank a small sip.

I stripped off my clothes and yanked on her leash. "Take me in your mouth, like a good girl."

"Yes, Sir."

Jesus! The only thing better than my wife's skilled lips wrapped around my dick were her lips around my dick with fizzing champagne bubbles on her tongue. It felt like a sizzling explosion as she careened her tingly mouth up and down my shaft.

Suddenly, she let go of my cock, took the champagne, and trickled it over my bulging erection.

"You bad girl. Look at the mess you made."

"I better clean it up, so I don't get punished." Her eyes filled with wicked admiration as my thick column was presented before her. I never grew tired of seeing her astonishment of how large of I was. It made me swell even more fully with veiny, rigid pride.

She descended on my bubbling tower with fierce determination. *Christ!* She was fantastic. Tugging on the leash only fueled her fire for my frothing cock flesh. She worked me over like a guzzling, slutty fiend. I fucking loved it, but put a stop to it before I popped my cork in her mouth. All of my cum tonight was meant for her ass.

I slithered my pulsating dick out of her mouth. "That's enough. Where did I tell you I was fucking you tonight?"

"My ass, Sir."

"That's right. I'm fucking you until you're good and sore." I leaned down and kissed her forehead. "Face down, ass in the air. Show me what's mine."

She turned over and presented me with her erotic playground. I smoothed my fingertips down her back, loving the feel of her satiny skin. "Good girl. Stay just like that."

I took my time heading to one of our kink drawers, retrieving lube, the vibrating egg, and remote, wondering how long it would take Nia to either touch herself or inquire about when she could come. Surprisingly, she was silent and still. Maybe our evening of Kamasutra show-and-tell had a profound effect on her.

My gaze lingered over her submission to me. Absolute beauty flowed out of her very soul. Somehow in that moment, I loved her even more. My gorgeous, sweet girl. My Nia.

"Baby, look at me." She raised her head. "Thank you for giving me your trust, and for giving me you. I love you."

"I love you too. And, I want you... I mean, would you..." She sighed in frustration.

"What do want, sweetie? Tell me."

She looked me right in the eye. "I want you to push me, like Emma. I want you to push my limits."

"As you wish, my angel. But, don't be afraid to use your safe word. Agreed?"

"Agreed, Sir." She resumed her pose, with her head down.

How did I get so fucking lucky? The girl of my dreams was also a whore for my cock. She was the entire package and everything I thought I would never find. Before I met her, I had almost given up on relationships. But then Nia walked into my life, or should I say, spun, and shook it up—shook me up. She made me feel alive. That was why I fought for her and with her. I never gave up. No matter what, I would spend the rest of my life loving this beautiful women offering herself to me. I was going to take her. Take her as I pleased, right now.

I knelt down behind her, setting the lube and egg close by. "I bet I know a good girl that would like to come." I fileted open her saturated folds, inhaling her scent. She smelled like heaven. Her body bowed like a kitten in heat for the first time. She had an endless appetite for sex, and tonight I would feed her hunger.

The flat of my tongue licked from her clit to her puckered opening. My girl tasted so sweet. I feasted on every bit of her until her body percolated and hummed. Then, I remembered how incredible the champagne bubbles felt on my cock. I slipped two fingers inside her to keep her amped up and took a swig from the bottle.

"Spread yourself nice and wide for me, baby."

Her juicy lady meat was on display, so accessible. I buried my face into her pussy and shook my head vigorously. She rewarded me by drenching my face in her wetness.

"Oh ... the champagne, it ... ah ... tingles."

My fingers rubbed and tapped her clit. "Do you like it? Do you want more?"

"Yes. I want more, Sir."

I poured the *Veuve Clicquot* directly on her butt, and into her crack. She squealed and convulsed in pleasure. Then I lapped it up like a thirsty madman, drunk off her special cocktail of champagne and nectar-like fluids.

When she neared the fringe of orgasm, I slowed down. Normally, she would have protested, but Nia was so obedient for me. The softest cries sounded in her throat as I reached for the vibrating egg. I gently pushed it inside her pussy and turned to the lowest setting. Her hips churned in approval. I applied a thick layer of lube over my dick and pressed it to her snuggest hole.

The tip slipped in, and Nia instantly squirted all over the carpet. "Oh fuck," she cried. My girl loved it in the ass. "Yes! Ah... Oh, my fucking Christ."

I stuffed in the next few inches and sawed her tight tunnel, easy and slow. "You're such a good girl. You feel... Fuck ... you feel so good, baby."

"You feel so fucking huge... Ah... Oh... Can I touch myself...? I feel like I'm going to come again."

I spanked her bottom. "No. My greedy little slut will have to wait."

She whimpered in agony. "Yes, Sir. Oh ... God."

My hand dug into her cheeks, grabbing handfuls of bum flesh as I impaled her sweet ass further. I let her adjust to my girth before rocking her with fluid, more forceful strokes. *Christ.* Her anal walls squeezed my cock so fucking hard. Her body trembled and begged for more. I skewered her with all my length, and she screamed in acceptance as pain and pleasure melted together.

This was a next-level ass fuck. I reached for the leash and jerked her to me, with my other hand gripping her chin. "Do you want it harder? Tell me."

Her lustful eyes met mine. "Yes. Harder. Fuck me in two."

My mouth came down on hers, showering her with my burning need, and my intense desire to claim her more fully than ever. I released her mouth and clutched her throat. She gasped as I guided her head face down on the floor.

I let go of her leash, latched onto her wrists and fucked her ass like a boss. Each thrust speared her clenching hole with sharp, grueling strokes. My balls slapped against her, spurring us to the edge of the cliff.

Freeing one wrist, I grunted, "Now... Oh, fuck. Now you can come. Touch yourself."

Her fingers flew to her clit while I wrapped her hair around my hand and tugged. Nia detonated on my command. Her body tremors were so strong that her rectum flared and corseted roughly around my cock, and I erupted a brutal, heavy load deep inside her.

I groaned, "Oh, Christ, fuck. Who is coming in your ass?"

She wailed in breathy moans, "My Sir. My ... Sir owns my ass. All my holes belong to you."

My cum overflowed and spilled down her crack. I kept fucking her until the very last drop and twitch.

When I released Nia's hair and wrist, her body buckled. Slowly I extricated myself out of her and carefully scooped her up onto my lap.

Her eyes appeared dazed, but the look on her face was pure peace. "Derek ... I—"

"Shh... Don't try to talk. Just stay right here, where you belong."

She burrowed her head in my chest. "I could stay in your arms forever."

I held her tight. "Forever and always."

Chapter Four

"Sweetie. I'm heading to the airport soon. Are you awake?"

The Japan morning of dread was here. I had to say goodbye to my angel. We were inseparable since the night of the "ass rapture," as Nia called it. Even though she was sore as hell, we played almost non-stop. Sven Smorgasbord, from the University of Toaster Strudel, also returned, indulging her in a Swedish massage that led to a game of mutual masturbation. We watched each other, and whoever held out the longest, won the oral prize. Or should I say, blowjob, because I won. What a piece of cake. Her pussy was like a house of cards. One false move and it folded.

She rubbed her eyes. "Thank you for waking me up. I wanted to see you off."

I sat on the bed. "That reminds me. No getting off until I get back. I insist."

"Really? It's like you just put my lady parts in jail."

"I should lock up the Viking and Buzz too, just not with you."

"I promise. I'll be good. I'm getting my period in a few days anyway."

"Looks like I'm getting out of town just in time. According to my calculations, you'll have PMS any minute now."

She jerked upright. "Oh my God. Did you plan your shoot around my cycle?"

"I'll never tell."

Nia flung a pillow at me. "Derek Pierce. You're awful."

Molly jumped onto the bed and barked.

"Wow. Both of my girls are giving me a hard time. I better get the hell out of here. But first, I have something for you." I reached under the bed and produced a *Prada* package.

"More *Prada*! Are you kidding me?"

"It's just a little something. To tide you over until Christmas."

She opened her gift. "Oh, these are crazy amazing! Julia asked for *Prada* sunglasses for Christmas. I better hide these until they get back from California or she'll be all jelly. I hope Phillip bought her a pair."

"That reminds me. There will be boxes delivered while I'm gone. It's your Christmas gifts. So no peeking, young lady, or you'll get coal in your stocking."

"Not a smidge of a peek. I want to be surprised. And when you get back, I'll have everything decorated. It's going to look like the North Pole exploded in the house."

"You don't have to go to all that trouble. Just the manger scene, and a tree and I'm good."

"Oh, Bah Humbug. What about your train? And Christmas stockings, and twinkle lights. I want it to look like a Winter Wonderland. I have a plan."

"Well, I didn't know there was a plan." My phone beeped. It was Jake, ready to take me to the airport.

Nia put her head down. "Do you have to go?"

"I'm afraid so. Come here." I drew her to my lap. "I'm going to miss you."

She sighed. "I'm going to miss you too."

I rubbed her back. "Do you want to go back to sleep or do you want me to get you something before I go?"

"I don't need a thing. Just you. I just need you to be safe and come back home."

"Of course. I wish I could put you in my pocket and take you with me."

I pressed my lips to hers, and when I pulled away, Nia gazed deep into my eyes. For a moment, there was something different in her angelic, sweet face that I'd never seen before.

She furrowed her brow. "Derek, what is it? Is something wrong?"

"No. Nothing. I don't know. If it's possible, you just got more beautiful right before my eyes. You're so beautiful." I cradled her in my arms and kissed the top of her head. "I haven't even left yet, and I already can't wait to come home."

* * * *

"Have there been any updates?" Jake appeared in the doorway, wearing a grim expression.

It was December 22 in Japan. The rain poured down so hard it clanged against the roof of my dingy makeshift office at the Sanin Kaigan National Park. The shoot in Japan was ahead of schedule until storms blew in, screwing up our last shot. It was the money shot, the cliffhanger, and one of the main reasons I decided to film on location.

"Keith is making some calls. He's also downloading an international weather app onto his phone since the local meteorologists are predicting different things."

"Are any of them predicting a clear sunset, because that's what we need?"

I stared at my desk with my head in my hands. "I don't know. This fucking sucks."

"We were supposed to be headed back to Vegas by now. What's your plan?"

"I have to get the shot. We'll stay, as long as it takes."

"Derek... Don't take this the wrong way, you know I'm grateful for the opportunities you've given me, but... Never mind I shouldn't say anything."

"No. Go ahead. I've always told you to be honest with me."

"Well ... it's just that... It's Christmas ... and..."

"I know. But, I can't think about that right now. We're going to get the shot, and that's all there is to it."

"What did Nia say?"

"About what?"

"About not heading back to Vegas yet."

"Actually, she was cool about it. What about Lacey?"

"She fucking freaked. She's afraid I'll miss her niece's christening."

"Lacey has a niece?"

"Yeah. Don't you remember? Her sister, Amy, had a baby right before Brooke and Tom's wedding. She showed you pictures at the rehearsal dinner."

"Oh, okay. Sorry. I forgot all about it."

"I may remind you of this when you have kids someday, and I forget their names."

"Fair enough. By the way, what's her niece's name?"

Jake shrugged. "I don't know. It's ... um ... Rose ... or ... Lilly... It's definitely a flower or something."

"Uncle Jake, you're really on top of things. I'll be sure to let Lacey know. I like the name, Lilly. It's Nia's favorite flower, and it was her mom's middle name."

"I'll make a deal with you. I won't tell Lacey you forgot she had a niece, if you don't tell her I forgot her niece's name."

"Deal. And I'm sorry we've been delayed. Who knows, we might get a lucky break in a couple of hours and nail this last scene."

"For all our sakes, I hope you're right. I'll catch you later."

Jake headed out, and my phone rang. It was my mom.

"Hey, Mom. I just talked to Dad this morning. Is everything okay?"

"We're fine."

"It's kind of late in Chicago."

There was a long pause. This wasn't good. When my mom paused, it meant she was going to let me have it. My sister, Dina, called it "the calm before the storm."

"Derek Charles Pierce, I'm so upset with you. I can't believe you're still in Japan. What about Nia, and your anniversary, and Christmas?"

Oh fuck, she used my middle name. "Mom, relax. Nia is fine. She understands. I'm going to get a weather update shortly. It's possible we could get the shot at sunset, and fly home late tonight."

"See that you do. I will not have my daughter-in-law spend Christmas alone. Do you remember when you were five, and your father got stuck in New York because he was working, and there was a blizzard?"

"Yeah, I remember. It was a rough Christmas, for all of us."

"He still regrets it. He talked about it after he hung up with you this morning. It's not worth it. Please, pack up the crew and go home right now."

"Mom, I can't do that. Dad's the one who told me to make this work. I already went over budget by shooting on location. I can't fuck up twice."

"You can't what?" she reprimanded.

"Sorry. I can't mess up twice."

"I'm going to call Nia in the morning..."

"Mom ... you're breaking up... Mom ... if you can hear me, I love you. I'll call you when I get back to Vegas."

Damn it. The phone went dead. The signal here was shit.

Keith came into my office glued to his phone. "This app is taking forever to download. The Wi-Fi is total crap."

"I know. My phone dropped out mid-conversation with my mom. Although, she was letting me have it, so it wasn't the worst thing in the world."

"Oh really? What did the great Valerie Elizabeth Bennett Pierce have to say? Did she take a long pause and then three name you?"

"Yeah. How did you know that?"

"She's been doing that since Junior High. Ever since you got caught making out with Tiffany Trent in the girl's locker room."

"It was much easier to talk my way out things back then. She's angry I'm still trying to get the last shot. She's worried about Nia. But, Nia's fine. She wasn't upset when I told her we got delayed."

"She will be upset if you don't make home in time for your anniversary." Keith glanced down and checked his phone. "Finally, the app loaded."

"Well, what's it say? Any chance the sun is coming out today?"

"Hang on." Keith sunk into the chair across from my desk. "Oh, hell no. I hope this is as bad at predicting the weather as I am at football. Rain until Christmas morning. Even with the time change, you won't make it back to Vegas for your anniversary on Christmas Eve. It's your call? What do you want to do? We could cut our losses and head back now? The longer we stay here, the more we go over budget."

"This is too important. We can't give up yet. I need time to think."

* * * *

"Hello? Nia?" It was the middle of the night in Japan. I was still here. The phone jolted me out of a dead sleep.

"Derek, it's Eden. Did I catch you at a bad time?"

Eden? It took me a second to fully wake up and realize my former fake girlfriend was on the phone. I hadn't spoken to her in months. Our past "for the cameras only" relationship seemed like a lifetime ago.

"It's the middle of the night in Japan. I was asleep."

"You're in Japan? Tomorrow is Christmas Eve. What the hell are doing in Japan?"

"Actually it's already Christmas Eve here. I'm shooting the finale of my new show. Eden, what's wrong? You sound like you've been crying."

"It's Heather. She left me."

"Oh, God, I'm sorry. What happened?"

"It's all my fault." She broke down for a moment, and got herself under control. "I'm sorry I woke you. I didn't know who else to call. Please, don't worry about me. Go back to sleep."

"No. It's fine. I'm up. Tell me about Heather."

"She ... she finally had enough. I was supposed to take a break in January, and I just signed on for guest starring role on, *The Secret Wives' Club*. It's a five episode arc. I've taken every single job I've been offered since I came out. I'm so afraid of not working again. I'm even doing TV."

"Oh, TV? You're really slumming with the rest of us now."

"You know what I mean. I used to take long breaks, and turn down work, and now I don't."

"Well, talk to me. Tell me what's going on. You're the highest paid female film actress in Hollywood. Why are you scared?"

She exhaled. "My last few movies bombed. And there's always someone younger, and prettier, not to mention heterosexual nipping at my heels. The paranoia ate me away. Heather kept begging me to slow down, to spend more time with her. You know how she hates the Hollywood scene."

"I do. She and Nia have always been on the same page about that. So, maybe Heather is just a little pissed. She'll get over it. Tell her you'll get out of the TV show, take her on a trip, something like that."

Her voice quivered. "I tried all of that. She says it's too late. Derek, she's gone. She packed up all of her stuff. She even took our dog, Marley. I'm all alone." She sobbed. "I've royally screwed everything up this time. Heather was the love of my life."

"Don't cry. You can still fix this. But, you're going to have to make some real changes and prove to Heather that she comes first. It's what I did with Nia."

"No you didn't," she sniffled with a snip to her voice. "It's practically Christmas and you're on the other side of the world, hoping to get one last great shot. Am I right?"

"I... Fuck, you know me too well. You're right. But Nia's been great about it."

"She won't be if you don't get home for Christmas. Derek, don't do what I've done. The most important person in my life has gone. And, I can't blame her for leaving. I made promises I didn't keep, all for the sake of one more job. It's not worth it. No shot is worth destroying what you have with Nia."

"I hear you. We just need a little break in the rain today, that's all. Everyone is counting on me. The network wants me to stay. It's a no-win situation if the sun doesn't come out today."

"Do what you have to do to get home to your wife."

"Message received. Are you going to be okay?"

"I honestly don't know. But, I'll let you go. Thanks for talking."

"Anytime. You know I'll always be here for you. I'll touch base soon."

"Thanks. Merry Christmas."

"It will be if you and Heather get back together, and we get a little sunshine."

* * * *

"Derek, what's it going to be?" Keith asked. "Are we staying?"

It was five hours later on Christmas Eve in Japan, and I was back in my shitty little cubby of an office, climbing the walls.

"Of course we're staying. It finally stopped raining. Is the sun out?"

"No, it's gloomy as hell out there. All the stations and my app say there's another storm system headed our way late this afternoon. It's supposed to be worse. Some of them are calling it a tsunami. This is bad."

"Not as bad if we come home without the shot, or if we have to fly everyone back here after the holidays. It will cost a fortune."

"Are you seriously going to make me tell everyone we aren't going home for Christmas?"

"We don't know that a hundred percent. There's still a chance that it won't blow through here until tomorrow, or at all."

"I think everybody has a right to know what the plan is. I've been trying to keep this from you, but the cast and crew are pissed. I guess I'm lucky since Tim is here, but everyone else is missing their families. Madison was in tears this morning."

I pounded my fist on the desk. "Fuck. This is exactly what I don't need to hear."

"I'm sorry. But, you know I always give it to you straight. I wouldn't be doing my job if I didn't tell you."

"Of course, and I appreciate it, but everybody knew this was a possibility. They all signed off on it. Even Madison. We talked about this before she took the part, and now I'm the asshole. Well, that's just fucking great."

"Should I not have said anything?"

"No. You did the right thing. I guess someone has to be the bad guy, and I suppose it should be me. Go tell everyone we are staying until I get the shot I want, and it probably won't be until after Christmas, and if they have a problem with it, they can come see me."

"You got it. Let's just hope they don't shoot the messenger."

"If anyone gives you shit, remind them they're being paid to sit on their asses and stay in a five-star hotel." I checked my phone. "Fuck. It's another message from a network exec. I feel like telling everyone to go to hell."

"Look, Derek, the last thing I want to do is piss you off, but I have to be honest. Are you sure this is the right move? Just take a second, and think about this. Think about Nia."

"I've been thinking about nothing else for three days now, non-stop. Do you have any idea the pressure I'm under? I have my Dad's voice in my head saying, 'make this work,' and 'family first.' How the fuck am I supposed to do both?"

"What can I do to help?"

I put my head in my hands and exhaled. "Just tell them ... we're staying."

Keith took tentative steps toward my desk. "Would it be okay to give everyone their Christmas gift? The *Prada* sunglasses?"

"Sure. That's not a bad idea. And maybe contact the hotel, and see if we can throw together some kind of Christmas party tonight." I picked up my phone to check the signal. "I'm going to call Nia and let her know."

"Okay. Later boss." Keith hurried out the room.

I punched in her number, knowing I was about to tell Nia something she didn't want to hear. But, she'd been such a good girl since I'd been here, and completely understanding so far.

"Hello... Derek?"

"Hi. How's my sweet girl?"

"Missing you. I kept my phone next to me. I was hoping you were going to call. Are you on the plane, are you coming home?"

"No, baby. I'm not. And it doesn't look good."

"What? I–I ... don't understand... What doesn't look good?"

"Me. Making it home for Christmas."

"You're not coming?"

"It doesn't look that way right now. This damn weather is fucking everything up."

Her voice cracked. "But ... it's Christmas ... and..." She cried softly, "I can't believe you're not coming. Tomorrow's our wedding anniversary."

God Damn it. I hated this. The sound of my girl's tears ripped me in two. "Angel, I know. This is killing me too. You know I'd be on my way in a second if I could."

"But can't you? Aren't you in charge? Can't you decide to come home?"

"It's not that simple. Everyone is counting on me."

She sobbed. "I was counting on you too."

"Shh... Baby, don't cry. I'll make this up to you. When I get home, we'll do Christmas for three days if you want. We can even renew our vows. Would you like that?"

"Yes ... but..."

"But what...? What is it?"

Her voice trembled and she hesitated. "Nothing... I was just thinking... If you're not coming, maybe Molly and I should go to California with Julia and Phillip. They chartered a plane so they could take Coco and Sammy. They're leaving in a little while."

I jumped out of my chair and headed to the window. "Are you still there?"

"Yes. You're breaking up a little, but I can hear you."

"It did stop raining for now. I know I said it didn't look good, but there's still a chance. I'd hate for you to go to California if I'm able to make it back. I just need more time."

"How much more time?"

"Five or six hours, at least. I should know something more definite in seven hours at the most."

"Derek, I can't ask them to wait that long."

"Well, can't you take a flight out later tonight?"

"No. I'm not leaving Molly or putting her in cargo like a suitcase. If I don't go with them, and you don't make it back... I–I'll be ... alone ... j–just Molly ...and m–me..." She broke down again.

"But you can't leave. Sweetie, I just need more time."

"You ... d–don't ... understand.... I–I ... have to..." She wept uncontrollably.

Hearing her like this was like taking a punch in the gut. I wanted nothing more than to wrap her up in my arms. "You have to what, baby? Try to calm down and talk to me."

She caught her breath. "I–I have to... I–I have something to tell you. I–It's ... important ... and..."

Out of the blue, Ali, Madison's stunt double, bounded in the room and hugged me. "Derek, thank you so much. I love *Prada*!"

Oh fuck! "Hang on, sweetie, two seconds," I said to Nia. "Ali, I'm on the phone. I'll have to talk to you later."

"Sorry. I just wanted to say thanks for the sunglasses. And Keith said there was a party tonight. I'm so excited."

I showed her to the door. "You're welcome." I practically had to push her out of my office. "Nia ... baby ... are you still there?"

"Yes, I'm here," she snapped. "And I heard everything. *Prada* sunglasses? And a party? Are you fucking kidding me?"

"It's not the way it sounded. I can explain."

"You can save it. I don't want to hear it. I feel like I'm in a fucking nightmare. Only now it's worse ... I—"

"Nia, stop. Don't go there."

"What do you expect me to do? What am I supposed to think after you tell me you're not coming home, but I should stay in Vegas, just in case, and then this bullshit with Ali. Were you going to tell me you're throwing a big party for everyone and giving the woman that was calling you the same sunglasses as me?"

"I gave the sunglasses to everyone for Christmas, not just her."

Her anger grew with every syllable she uttered. "Well, isn't that fucking awesome? I guess giving me a pair was just an afterthought. That's all I'll ever be—an afterthought."

"That's not true, and you know it."

"I feel like I don't know anything right now. I have to go. I need to call Julia."

"Nia, I told you. I just need more time. Don't leave Vegas. Promise me."

"Promise you?" she yelled. "Yeah, I'll promise you. You make promises all the time, and you don't keep them, so fine, I promise."

"Baby, please don't be like this."

"Like what? An emotional mess? You have no idea, not a fucking clue." Once again she broke down.

This tore me up inside. "Then tell me, angel. What's going on?"

"I can't," she wept. "Not like this. I have to go."

"Nia, don't."

The line went dead. *Fuck!* I nearly hurled my cell through the window. Instead, I called Nia back. *God Damn, voicemail.* She was doing it again. Shutting me out, cutting me off. The motherfucking phone. I kicked my chair across the room.

"Hey, is it safe to come in?" Ali peeked her head in the door.

I grabbed the chair and pushed it back into place. "Yeah. What now?"

She helped herself to a seat. "Well, about earlier. I didn't know you were on the phone when I came bursting into your office. I was just so excited about the sunglasses and the party. I wasn't paying attention. I'm really sorry I interrupted."

My mind raced with thoughts of Nia. I barely heard her while I stared out the window, willing the sun to come out. "Don't worry about it."

"I also wanted to tell you, that I'm glad were staying in Japan for Christmas. I think it'll be fun."

"I'm still hopeful it will stop raining this afternoon. Anyway ... I've got some calls to make." I walked to the door, and she took the hint and followed.

Before she left, she leaned against the wall. "Look, Derek, I know you're married, and I'm okay with that.

Just know I'm here for you, if you get lonely." She ran her hand over my chest. "I can be very discreet. It could be our little secret."

For a moment, my past flashed before my eyes. There was a time in my twenties I wouldn't have refused an offer like Ali's. Once, on set in Sweden, I had a fling with my sexy co-star, Pamela, and her stunt double, Kelsey, without either of them finding out. When I returned to the LA, we all got on with our lives like it never happened.

I was no longer that guy. That was the past. And although my present with Nia was a fucked-up mess, there wasn't a chance in hell I would jeopardize our future.

I carefully removed Ali's hand from my chest. "Ali, I want you to listen to me, so we're clear."

A look of delight crossed her face. "Oh, I'm listening."

"Good. You and I are never happening. And I expect you to conduct yourself at the party, and on set with a hundred percent professionalism, or I will fire you, and send you back to the States on a Greyhound Bus. Do you understand?"

Her mouth gaped open in shock. "I understand."

"Excellent. Go back to the holding room, and wait for instructions, and please don't come to my office again, unless the building is on fire. Got it?"

"Got it." She turned to go and stopped. "You know, you can't travel back to the States on a Greyhound bus."

"Exactly."

She'd be chewing on that one for a while. I hurried back to my desk and tried Nia again. It went straight to voicemail. There was no point leaving her a message. I walked outside and stared at the sky. Dark clouds loomed right over the cliff. God, I hoped they'd just keep rolling by. The thought of Nia crying made me feel like shit. What the hell couldn't she tell me over the phone? She was so emotional. What if someone from her past contacted her, like Nick's parents. *Damn it!* This was going to eat me alive until I got back to Vegas. I should try to call her again.

When I returned to my office, Jake was waiting for me. "So, I just got off the phone with Lacey. That was pleasant."

"I take from the sarcastic tone it didn't go well."

"I've never heard her so pissed and upset at the same time. One second she was crying, and then ripping me a new one. I don't blame her. She's at her parents' house, and they aren't big fans of mine to begin with."

"I had no idea. I'm sorry."

"How did things go with Nia?"

"Same. She hung up on me." When I glanced down at my phone, it gave me an idea. "Hey, do you think Lacey could call Nia for me and ask her to answer her phone. She won't take my calls."

"Sorry, man. I think you're the last person Lacey wants to do a favor for right now."

I sat on the edge of my desk. "You're probably right. Presently, I'm the most hated man in Japan and on American soil. I keep wondering if it's worth it?"

"Only you can answer that question. I don't envy you. I wouldn't want to be in your shoes. I'm going to head back to the holding room. You should know they've started to call it the holding cell."

"Holding cell? Who started it calling it that?"

Jake smirked. "Well, I may have started it. It's catching on."

"Thanks, buddy."

Over the next two hours, I felt like a pent-up animal pacing my office trying to reach Nia. She wouldn't answer her damn phone. How did we get here again? All those times she shut me out. My mind kept reliving the day I came home to broken glass, and her engagement ring lying on the kitchen counter, after she walked in on Mandy Hamilton and I rehearsing. It crushed me to let her go. Our breakup was the most painful time in my life. But, I put her through hell, and if I was going to get her back, I had to make it right. *The Alec Stone Chronicles* was supposed to fix everything. It was meant to show her she was first, my number one priority. *What the fuck had I done?*

I wasn't just blowing it with Nia. I felt like I was single-handedly stealing everyone's Christmas. All day long, cast and crew leered at me from the hallway. I was a holiday piranha. I couldn't even face Madison. We'd been friends and cast mates since season one of *First Bite*. The first season of that show ended with a big wrap party at the Beverly Hills Hotel, now this one was turning into a disaster.

I ventured outside for another check. Jesus, it looked worse. Deflated, I went back to my office and found Ray, my director of photography watching the small flat screen in the corner.

"Are you sure you want to be seen with me, Ray? I'm a wanted man. The Grinch who Stole Christmas."

"Hey, it's cool with me. I'd rather be working. Do you mind if I check some scores? The reception at the hotel is decent, but I can't get anything on my phone here."

"Help yourself. I've been trying to reach my wife all day since I told her the news. She's not taking my calls."

"Oh, I've been there, brother. It ain't ever going to get any better. Trust me."

"What do you mean?"

"You know. Issues with your wife. If they aren't in the business, they don't get it. Shit happens out of your control, you got to roll with it. You miss one soccer game they act like it's the end of the world. But you don't hear any complaints when you buy them a new car. You have to take the good with the bad."

"I appreciate that. Thanks. And I'm sorry about Christmas. I know you have kids."

"Don't sweat it. I wouldn't have gotten to see them anyhow. My ex has them, so I don't mind. I'm glad I'm working. I don't have anyone to go home to. That's the price you pay if you want to have a future in this business. My future might not be getting to see my kids as much, or being alone on Christmas, but, isn't that the way it is for everyone who's successful in Hollywood?"

"Well, I think you can have both."

He turned off the TV and stood. "Yeah, okay. You let me know how that works out, you know, if your wife ever takes your calls again. Good luck. You're going to need it."

He left and my phone vibrated. I hoped to God it was Nia, but it wasn't. It was a text message my mom sent hours ago that just popped up. Damn, she sent me a huge attachment. Before it opened, Jake rushed into the room.

He grabbed the remote. "Derek, you need to see this." He turned it to CNN International and cranked the volume.

The female reporter at the airport said, "Authorities will be closing Narita International and Haneda airports later tonight as tsunami-like conditions threaten to hit the area in just a matter of hours. At this point, they don't know when flights will resume. The only good news is the majority of holiday traffic happened yesterday, and today has been relatively light by comparison. I spoke to a ticket agent, and they said if you planned to fly out on Christmas morning get here now. They can hopefully find you a seat, because to repeat—once they close the airports they do not know when they will reopen, if this impending storm is as intense as predicted. Back to you."

Jake clicked the TV off. "Derek, there's no telling when we'll get out of here now. What do you want to do?"

My phone vibrated again, and I checked it. Mom's attachment downloaded. She sent pictures from my wedding. I looked down at this gorgeous picture of my Nia, her face so full of love for me. She beamed with hope and happiness. I made vows to her. I meant them. I wasn't going to let her down. "Let's get the hell out of here. Let's go home."

* * * *

"It shouldn't be much longer, Mr. Pierce. We've finally been cleared for takeoff." My pilot Brett said over my plane's intercom.

It took forever to get to the airport. The traffic was insane. Jake, Tim, Keith and I buckled up in the captain's chairs. We'd been sitting on the tarmac for hours.

"Did you get a hold of anyone from the network?" Keith asked. "Do they know we didn't get the last shot?"

I cracked open a beer. "Yeah. They aren't happy, but fuck 'em. At the end of the day, it was my call. After the holidays, we'll try to green screen it. If I'm not satisfied, I'm going to pay to reshoot it here."

Tim poured himself some red wine. "Well, for what it's worth, I think you did the right thing."

"Thanks, man. I think I did too."

"Hey, I just got a text from Lacey." Jake leaned forward and read it. "Tell Derek thank you. I'm so glad you're on the way. I did try to call Nia for him. It went to voicemail. I texted her and she didn't text back."

"I have a bad feeling." I took my phone out of my pocket and checked it once more. "She said she had something to tell me. Fuck, I wish we were landing instead of taking off. I have no idea if she's in Vegas or if she went to California."

"I'll text Lacey and tell her to keep trying to get a hold of Nia."

"Thanks. Hey … this is weird." I tapped on my screen. "I have a voicemail from Nia's office number."

"When did she call you?" Tim asked.

"I don't know." I held the phone to my ear. "Shit. I can't make out what she's saying. Why is she calling me from her office?" I hit the button for the speakerphone. "Can you guys understand any of this?"

I played the message for them. Keith shook his head. "I can't make out a thing. But, she called so take that as a good sign."

"Yeah. And we're headed home." Tim raised his glass and said in a very bad British accent. "God bless us, every one."

For the first time in days, I almost laughed. "Thank you, Tiny Tim."

Keith chimed in. "Wait. If you're Tiny Tim, who does that make me?"

Tim waved his hand in disgust. "The Ghost of Christmas Gas. Damn it, Keith Johnson, I know that was you."

"Oh fine. Blame the black guy," Keith joked.

This was going to be a long flight…

* * * *

By the time I made it to my front door on Christmas Eve, it was pitch-black, except for the stars in the sky. I slid my key into the lock. Please. Nia. Please still be here.

The door eased open. "Nia? Angel?"

Nothing. The silence in the house was deafening. I dropped my bag, and raced up the stairs. Maybe she was asleep. I threw open our bedroom door. "Sweetie?"

She wasn't there. I dashed through the rest of the rooms, calling for her and Molly. But, I was too late. The house was empty. They were gone. *Fuck!* I blew it. I really blew it. She was counting on me and I let her down.

I trudged downstairs with my heart in my throat, unable to get the sound of Nia crying out of my mind. God, I'd give anything to hold her right now. When I got to the kitchen, I didn't even flip on the light. I sank down into a chair at the table, with my head in my hands. *Damn it. Why didn't I leave Japan sooner?* The thought of Nia bawling her eyes out at Julia's house in California was so hellish, I felt sick.

I lifted my head and stared into the darkness, until a small beam of light caught my eye. It was coming from the TV room. I shoved myself out my chair to get a closer look. It was the manger scene, glowing in soft white lights just like it did a year ago when we got married. If only I could turn back time and make this right I would... *Wait ... my girl wouldn't have gone to California and left those lights on.*

I flew into room at breakneck speed and skidded to a halt. *Oh, thank God.* She didn't leave. She was here. My Nia was curled up on the couch, sound sleep, wearing her red and green candy cane pajamas. The sight of her, almost made my knees buckle in sweet relief.

"Baby?" I rushed to her side, and gently woke her. "Nia?"

Her eyes flipped open. "Derek? Am ... I dreaming? You're ... home?"

"Yes. Angel. I'm home." She folded into me, and I held her tight.

"You're here? You're really here?" She peeked up at me with sleepy eyes.

"Yes, sweetie, I'm really here." I clutched her to my chest. "I've going been crazy trying to reach you. When you didn't answer your phone, I thought you'd left."

"You didn't get my message?"

"I got a voicemail from your office number, but I couldn't understand a word you said. Jesus, I've been worried sick."

"I'm so sorry. I was trying to tell you I wasn't going to California, and what happened to my phone. Please don't be angry."

"Hey." I clasped her face in my hands. "It's my fault we were in this hell to begin with. I'm the one that should be apologizing. What's going on with your phone?"

"I got so mad when you said you weren't coming home, I threw it. It busted."

"Like, you cracked it and couldn't get it to work?"

"No, like it's in a million tiny pieces. I guess I don't know my own strength."

"My girl has quite an arm." I brushed my fingertips over her cheek. Was it possible she became even more beautiful while I was gone? "God, I missed you so much." I pressed my lips to hers for a tender kiss. "Hmm ... you smell so good." My mouth made a trail from her jawline to her neck. "I could just devour you right here."

Nia teased. "Mmm... You just want me for my mac and cheese."

I chuckled mid-nibble. "You made mac and cheese? As in Aunt Mary Jane's mac and cheese?"

"Yup. It's extra cheesy too."

"And Molly? Where is she?"

As if on cue, Molly bounded into the room, and jumped on the couch in between us. "Hey, there's my pooch." She lapped at my face while I gave her ears a scratch.

"She missed you almost as much as I did. I gave her some new toys for Christmas. She destroyed half of them, and dragged the other half to her hoarder tree."

Molly eyed a toy that was only semi-demolished. She hopped off my lap, grabbed it, and whisked it outside. Nia giggled. "There she goes. Another one bites the dust."

It was then I took a good look around the Winter Wonderland Nia created. "The house looks great. And, you … you look so cute in your Christmas pajamas. I can't believe you did all this after... I was so worried I blew it after you hung up."

"Well, you totally did. And when I heard Ali's voice, it took me to a bad place. But, then I calmed down and realized there were so many times you were the only one keeping the faith, and believing in us. This time, it was my turn. I didn't run. I had faith in you and in what we have. In my heart, I knew you were coming home. I just wished I figured that out before I smashed my phone to bits. I'm so sorry. That's not how I planned our anniversary."

"That's right. It's not quite midnight. I made it just in time. Happy anniversary. Come here." I pulled her to my lap. "So, Mrs. Very Married Nia Pierce. What was your plan?"

"It doesn't matter now." Tears sprang to her eyes. "I'm starting to think plans are overrated."

"Why would you say that...? Hey... you're crying." I wiped her tears away with the back of my hand. "You said on the phone you had something to tell me. Please, talk to me."

More tears spilled down her cheeks, and she hung her head. "Derek... I–I..."

I tucked my finger under her chin. "Baby, eyes on me. You can tell me anything."

She swallowed hard. "Derek ... I'm... I'm...pregnant."

All the air left my lungs. "What? Are you sure?"

She squirmed off my lap, moved to her knees, and rambled. "Yeah. I just went to the doctor. My period never came, and I mentioned it to Julia, and you know how she is. She pulled some strings and got me an appointment with her gyno. I peed on a stick, did some blood work, and I was like, son of a bitch, I'm pregnant."

My head spun in circles. "I–I ... don't understand. You're on the pill."

"Apparently the only birth control that works a hundred percent of the time is abstinence, which you and I are not fans of. Plus, the doctor said maybe being sick threw my system out of whack."

I was so paralyzed by the news. I couldn't speak.

"Derek ... I know this is a shock. It still is for me too, and I've had a couple of days to let it sink in. Are you mad? Please, say something."

When I gazed into my girl's beautiful dark eyes, the shock vanished and was replaced with some sort of indescribable happiness I couldn't express. I grappled to find the right words. "Nia, of course I'm not mad. I–I'm ... fucking ecstatic. This is... It's ... the most ... perfect thing you could have ever told me." I placed my hands on her stomach. "This is real. This is really happening. We're going to have a baby?"

She nodded, choking back tears. "Yes. We're going to have a baby."

"I love you so much."

"I love you too."

I swept her into my arms, and our mouths joined together as one. In that second, our deep connection that had been there since the day I laid eyes on her intensified to a new place. Three little words, she only said three little words, "Derek, I'm pregnant," and it was as if someone opened up a part of my heart I didn't know was there.

I immersed myself in every inch of her, vowing I would learn from the past, make the most of every moment in the present, and spend the future loving her more fully.

The clock on the wall chimed. It was midnight.

Nia listened to the soft bell tones and glanced up at the manger scene. "It's Christmas."

I smoothed the hair off her face, in awe of my girl. "It is. Merry Christmas, sweetie."

"Merry Christmas, Derek."

I leaned down and kissed her belly. "I still can't believe it. We're going to be parents."

"We're going to be a real family."

"Baby, we already are." I took my hands in hers, and held them, just like the day of our wedding. "Nia you've always been my family. You're the love of my life, my angel, my home."

THE END

One Year Later…

"Is she still asleep?" I drew back the covers and climbed into bed.

"Yeah. She had quite a night." Nia kissed her forehead and settled in next to me.

Lilly Elizabeth Pierce was born on September 4, weighing just over six pounds. I didn't think there was a more precious sight than my pregnant Nia, until I saw her holding our baby girl for the first time.

"Hey, why don't you give me the baby monitor? I'll put it on my nightstand, and if she wakes up, I'll take care of her."

"Are you sure?"

"Of course. You must be exhausted."

She handed me the monitor with a devilish grin. "Thank you. I had quite a night myself. Is it possible becoming a mother has made me even hornier? Since Naked Thanksgiving, I've been—"

"Insatiable. I'm beginning to think your launch sequence has a hair trigger."

"Are you complaining, Mr. Pierce?"

"Not a chance, Mrs. Very Married Nia Pierce. That was a long six weeks after Lilly was born." I wrapped my arms around her. "But, totally worth it. Lilly is perfect. She's just like you. We're so lucky."

Nia nestled into her spot. "We are lucky. Lilly and me. We're lucky to have you. I love you. This was the best anniversary and Christmas Eve. Thank you so much."

"Thank me for what?"

"For being here. For being home."

"There's no place I'd rather be, than with my girls." Molly raised her head from the end of the bed. "Yes, Molly, that includes you."

"She's been great with Lilly, hasn't she?"

"Yeah. She really has." I checked the clock. "Hey, it's midnight. Merry Christmas, angel."

"Merry Christmas."

I kissed the top of her head. "Goodnight, my sweet girl, I love you."

Within moments, my three girls were fast asleep. Molly was at the foot of the bed, Lilly in her crib, and my beautiful Nia, in my arms. They were my whole world. Everything I loved was in this room. *I'm never letting go...*

Author Biography

Rosemary grew up in Pennsylvania, one of six children. Her parents, Charles, and Dorothy, always supported all her creative endeavors, from acting to singing to Erotic Novelist. Yes, they are super cool.

She's been living in Las Vegas for over eighteen years with her husband Bill Johnson and their rescued pooch Harley.

In addition to writing, she also teaches ten fitness classes a week. Her limited spare time is usually spent at home with her hubby enjoying a home cooked, healthy meal and all things HBO and Netflix. When she ventures out to a restaurant, she normally splurges on her favorite dish, Mac and Cheese. It's just like Nia says in, *Running Away to Home*, "Sometimes it's good to be bad!"

ROSEMARY WILLHIDE

WWW.LUMINOSITYPUBLISHING.COM